I Heart Mr. Collins

Phoebe Braddock's Love Story

L. STARLA

Author's Note

This book contains coarse language, strong sexual references, non-monogamous relationships, drug use, and some depictions of sexual violence. Reader discretion is advised.

Dedication

—To Jason, who like a muse, ignited the spark of
spirit deep within.

Epigraph

"My passions, concentrated on a single point, resemble the rays of a sun assembled by a magnifying glass: they immediately set fire to whatever object they find in their way."
—MARQUIS DE SADE

Soundtrack

Some of these songs are referenced directly, while others fit the theme and mood of the story:

"Big Sky" by John O'Callaghan
"Rapture" by iio, Nadia Ali
"Oops!... I did It Again" by Britney Spears
"Lady-Hear me Tonight" by Modjo
"American Dream" by Jakatta
"God is a DJ" by Faithless
"Touch Me" by Rui Da Silva feat. Cassandra
"Take me Away" by 4 Strings
"Age Ain't Nothing But a Number" by Aaliyah
"Something" by Lasgo
"As the Rush Comes" by Motorcycle
"U Got It Bad" by Usher
"Lady Marmalade" by Christina Aguilera, Lil' Kim, Mýa,
       P!nk
"You Give Me Something" by Jamiroquai
"The Sound of Goodbye" by Armin van Buuren
"Man on the Run" by Dash Berlin, Cerf Mitiska, Jaren
"Bass, Beats & Melody" by Brooklyn Bounce
"I'm Afraid I Think I'm Human" by Sonicanimation
"I Feel Loved" by Depeche Mode
"Love Comes Again" by Tiësto, BT

Playlist available on Spotify.

Prologue

Diary Extract Dated Monday 14th February 2000

I'm so glad I have this diary to confide in because I reckon even Denise would think my latest crush is pretty tragic. Recently I have become aware of just how much I really, really want Mr. Collins, my 40yr old English teacher. I know a few of the other girls think he's cute, but that's mostly the old-school British accent and charm, which is only a part of what drives me wild. I also share a love of literature with him that will often get us talking outside of class. Plus, I find his scruffy brown hair and cheeky smile accented by dimples extremely hot. Oh my God- that smile!

Lately it seems like he has been smiling directly at me more than normal. Perhaps this is because of how much I find myself staring at him in class, hoping to draw his gaze. After today I wonder if the feeling is mutual because when he handed back my assignment he actually said, 'Happy Valentine's Day, Phoebe,' under his breath. I thought I was hearing things at first! Who says that to their student? It gives me hope that maybe one day, when I am no longer his student, I might be in luck.

After recently looking back through my diary and taking a journey down memory lane, I decided to write a more detailed account of the events leading up to my marriage. It is my hope that this memoir will help both me and my descendants understand the lifestyle choices I made and to forgive what some may consider indiscretions.

Chapter One

Diary extract dated Thursday 12th April 2001

'You are eighteen years of age now, yes?'

'Yes I am.'

'Would you object to me taking this any further?' He asked this last question while gliding his hand under my school dress and up along my inner thigh.

Smiling I replied, 'I would not object.'

That happened on the last day of term one, during my final year of high school. Because I had repeated a year in my early schooling, I was already eighteen years old, a legal adult in Australia.

The morning started out much as any other at the breakfast bar with my Mum, Laura Braddock.

'Morning Mum.'

'Morning Phoebe.' She kissed me on the cheek, then

3

handed me the milk. 'You were up late last night. How'd you go with that media studies project?'

'Finished, thank God. It's due in first period. We focus on TV media next term.'

'Ah good.' Smiling she added, 'Perhaps I'll get a chance to read a fresh paper again, and not dig them out of your room days later.'

I just gave her a guilty smile in response before plunging into my bowl of cereal.

'I spoke to your dad last night by the way. Plans are set for your stay there.'

'Thanks Mum. I was getting worried.' For as long as I could remember it had just been Mum and me. Dad left when I was a toddler and Mum had never remarried, claiming that she wanted to focus on motherhood rather than stepping back into the dating realm. I suspected that this had more to do with her fear of men hurting her again than she'd ever admit. She chose not to divulge the nature of her breakup with Dad to me because she did not want to sabotage my relationship with him. I typically only saw Dad for a few days during school holidays when time allowed for me to take a trip out to the country where he lived. Half the time he would even cancel those visits because he would decide to take-off on some wild voyage at the last minute, using the excuse of conducting important research for his writing. He was Tobias K. Braddock, successful fantasy adventure author;

something I could admire him for at least.
When I was able to see him, we had a lot of fun and
I loved that he indulged my own passion for books.
Some of my fondest childhood memories were of
Dad reading me the works of Enid Blyton as
bedtime stories. In my early teens I began compiling
my own library of rare edition books from across a
range of genres, but my most prized pieces were the
paperbacks that I had folded over and read to bits.
In more recent years my reading tastes had
changed, shifting into the realms of classic and
gothic romance. Jane Austen, Anne Radcliffe, and
the Brontë sisters stood out as favourites to me at
this time. Something about the plight of their
heroines struck chords with me and gave me the
vicarious means I needed to experience passionate
love.

Mum handed over my lunch bag then kissed me
farewell on the cheek before heading off to work. I
gave the contents of the bag a quick glance and sure
enough she had loaded it with a selection of my
favourite healthy foods, including sushi, carrot
sticks, yoghurt, and fruit salad.

ഇരു

When I boarded the bus, my best friend Denise
stood up and waved for me to join her. She gave me
a hug when I reached her, then as we sat, she
remarked, 'Oh my god I love your hair Phoebs! It's

so straight and shiny. And is that a Gucci fragrance you're wearing?'

I carefully placed my school bag down to ensure that it would not fall over before replying, 'Spot on hun, it's Gucci—my new fave! Thanks for noticing my hair—I straightened it today.' While I don't consider myself particularly vain, I do take some care to ensure my appearance is neat. Placing my head on Denise's shoulder I added, 'Let me guess, you're wearing a Dior today?'

'Hole-in-one babe! You are getting good at this. Oh wow—school break is about to start. I am way-excited! The gang have got some pretty wild parties planned for the next two weeks and—'

'Well H-E-L-L-O ladies!'

A couple of guys broke her thread of conversation as they took their seats across from us. They were in the unmistakable uniform of St. Mark's College, the posh Catholic school down the road from our own. They both wore black dress pants, white shirts, black blazers with red trim, and ties of black and red stripes.

The boy who greeted us, a very attractive looking jock with spiked up hair, turned to his friend briefly to add, 'See Nick, catching the bus isn't so bad.' Returning to smile at us both he made the introductions, 'So, I'm Curtis and this here is my mate, Nick. You'll have to excuse his mood today; he's just been grounded and misses his beloved car.'

He gave Nick a friendly nudge, which had the strange effect of easing the guy's mood.

Grinning and returning the nudge Nick replied, 'Hi ladies. You'll have to excuse my mate, Curtis; he can be quite rude at times.'

Denise, obviously flattered by the attention and unable to take her eyes off Curtis, introduced us both in her usual fashion, using exaggerated hand gestures. 'Well, it's a pleasure to meet you both. I'm Denise.' She placed both hands against her chest, ensuring attention was adequately drawn to where she thought it ought to go. 'And this is Phoebe.' She finished, placing both hands on my shoulder.

I loved Denise, she had always been a kind, loyal, and generous friend ever since I was seven years old, but her attention-seeking behaviour and model-like body meant that most boys overlooked me. My own physique was quite petite, being only five-foot-three with an A cup bra, and I chose to keep my natural dark brown hair colour rather than bleaching it blonde like Denise.

Denise leaned slightly forward towards Curtis and continued, 'Judging by your black and red uniforms I'm guessing you both go to St. Mark's?'

Curtis responded by leaning towards Denise. 'A most accurate observation, but now you have me at a disadvantage because I can't guess what school you go to.'

It was Nick who replied to this, sitting back casually

and smiling at me. 'You must be blind, Curtis! The logo on their blazers and bags is from St. Teresa's.' The focus of Nick's attention was not lost on me, and I felt compelled to return his smile. It was a captivating look thanks to his deep ocean-blue eyes that made me feel lost at sea. The effect was such that I was only vaguely aware that Denise and Curtis continued to converse. I took in all of Nick's facial features, from his honey-blond hair in a classic pompadour style, to his full lips and chiselled jawline, but it was those attentive eyes that drew me back into my trance. I was not lifted from my reverie until the boys reached their stop, but Curtis had made a point of giving us both his mobile number before parting; a gesture that Denise was all too happy to reciprocate.

ෆⓈⓇ

St. Teresa's was a relatively large girls' Catholic college on the East side of the city that adjoined the grand old cathedral sharing the same name—a favourite feature of mine. I was never devoutly religious, but I loved attending school mass in this Baroque-revival building, complete with a colonnade of columns decorated with gilded scrolls, intricate stain-glass windows, and a ceiling that seemed as high as the sky. It was such a contrast to the little suburban church that Mum took me to on Sundays.

Every school day started with home group and this year we had Mr. Collins supervising us for this fifteen-minute period; a bonus for me because he was my favourite teacher. Initially, this was because he had also been my English teacher and netball coach every year since I started high school, but over the last fifteen months I had been crushing on him too. During this session Mr. Collins reminded us that the end of term assembly, followed by an early dismissal would replace our afternoon lessons. After the morning formalities finished, he proceeded to share his news, 'Now ladies I wanted to inform you of this before they announce it in the afternoon's assembly. I will not be returning to teach at St. Teresa's next term. I am transferring to St. Mark's college for the remainder of the year, and this will likely become a permanent posting.'

An audible sigh of disappointment filled the classroom. I did not join this chorus, however, because I was sitting in stunned silence. I could almost feel tears welling up and it took all my inner strength to maintain composure. This man had been like a rock to me for so many years and he was leaving just at the pinnacle of my school education. I didn't know what to do or say; so, I just moved on to my next class despondently.

After my first lesson finally finished, I hurried to the library for my free period where I relaxed with the last of my current English reader, *Chocolat* by

Joanne Harris. The movie adaptation of this book had just come out and I was looking forward to an excursion with my English class to see it in the cinema next term. As soon as I remembered this, I dropped my book at the realisation that a new English teacher might not honour this promise made by Mr. Collins. I closed my eyes in quiet contemplation and tried some deep breathing to keep my calm. I don't know how long I remained in this state of meditation, but the recess bell brought me back to reality, so I jumped up to join my friends in our usual spot.

෨෭

The following study periods and lunch passed by with little incident or time for pensiveness and then it was assembly. The whole thing dragged on in the usual fashion of presentation after presentation. Then the dreaded announcement came at the end. The Principal, Mrs. Caldwell, explained that Mr. Collins would be transferring to St Mark's and that the whole school community would greatly miss him. She then called for a round of applause to thank him for his work and to wish him well in his future endeavours. At this, the whole student body, myself included, gave him a standing ovation and as I looked around, I saw tears on a few other cheeks as well.

After the assembly Denise and I grabbed a drink

from the canteen before heading back to our lockers to collect our bags.

Most of the crowd had died down by this stage, so we found ourselves alone in the corridor just outside our homeroom when Denise broached the topic of Mr. Collins, 'It'll be a shame to see Mr. Collins go. He was always my fave and an awesome netball coach to boot.'

At this I replied, 'I agree wholeheartedly, Denise. I'm really gonna miss him too, and his cheeky smile. I'll admit that I've had a huge crush on him for a while now.'

No sooner had these words left my mouth than Mr. Collins came walking out of the open door of our homeroom and approached us, giving me quite the surprise. I blushed, wondering if he heard what I said. 'Hello ladies. Phoebe, can I have a word please?'

He gestured for me to step inside the homeroom, which also doubled as his office. I bid Denise farewell with a coy smile, indicating that I would catch up with her soon, then promptly followed Mr. Collins' instructions. He closed and locked the door upon my entrance, and I stood blinking at him, uncomprehending. His gaze fixed on me intently with fierce longing eyes and then it dawned on me.

Gesturing to the hallway, I began to speak, 'Did you hear—'

His own words cut me off as he drew closer,

'While it saddens me to leave this school, I no longer feel the need to hold back from doing this.' At that he threw his arms around me, grabbing my backside, and kissed me deeply.

I started at first, but then I lifted my hands up, resting them behind his neck, and returned the kiss. I had kissed a few boys during my adolescent years, but this was altogether different. The scratchy stubble on his face, the scent of Old Spice cologne, and the way his tongue caressed my mouth, providing strong contrast to remind me that this man was much older and more experienced.

He pressed my body back toward his solid oak desk and I felt my backside resting against the edge of it. He lifted me up, seating me on it, and continued to kiss me for a few more minutes.

Then it happened.

When Mr. Collins eventually emptied himself inside me, he grunted, and we both collapsed onto the desk. I curled up in his arms and listened to his quick, shallow breaths.

He broke the silence first, 'I am going to give you my home address. Will you call upon me Phoebe?'

'Yes, I'd love to Mr. Collins.'

'Please, call me Jonah when we are alone.' Mr. Collins stood up and quickly dressed and I followed suit. He wrote his mobile number and address on a scrap of paper, then handed it to me, asking me to visit him soon. 'We had best be going now. I do not want to arouse any suspicions.'

We parted with a kiss as fiery as its predecessors and I soon found myself hopping along cloud nine all the long bus ride home.

Chapter Two

An empty wine glass tipped and rolled to the floor amidst the flurry of excited undressing. He had gone from composed and aloof one moment to ravaging me the next, pausing only when it came time to remove my dress and comment, 'Your choice of attire is very effective tonight my dear, whether intended or not.'

As much as I loved spending time with my family and attending church to celebrate Good Friday, I felt the day drag because I really wanted to see Mr. Collins again. Our encounter after school on Thursday ignited some intense emotions within me, uncovering a more impulsive side that I had never known before. When I had some quiet time to myself on Thursday night and Friday, I kept replaying the mental footage of what seemed like an unreal fantasy, but the scrap of paper with his contact details was proof that it was all real. The first thing I did when I woke (somewhat late) on Saturday morning was reach over to my phone and call Mr. Collins.

'Good morning, Jonah Collins speaking.'

Just hearing his voice sent shock waves through my body. 'Hi Mr. Collins, it's Phoebe.'

I could hear an audible intake of breath on his end of the line. 'Morning Phoebe, I am so glad you called. How are you?'

I really had to avoid the urge to spurt out everything I was thinking and feeling in that moment, so reminding myself to stay calm, I continued, 'I'm good thanks. How are you?'

'I am well, thank you… Did you…enjoy Good Friday?'

I wondered who would get to the point first. 'Yes, I did. After church Mum hosted a nice dinner for our extended family.'

'That sounds lovely…Do you have much planned for the rest of the Easter weekend?' He was finally getting somewhere.

'Well, I will be going to church again tomorrow and then visiting Dad for the rest of the weekend, but I don't have any plans for today.'

'Perhaps you would…um… like to…' (*Wow, in all these years I had never heard Mr. Collins, Oxford doctorate in English literature, so unsure of his words*). '…visit me this evening?'

There, it was out at last. I could barely contain my excitement, so I paused a moment before replying. 'I would love to. What time?'

I could almost hear his sigh of relief. 'Shall we say seven?'

'Seven it is.' *I may have been a little too enthusiastic there.*

'Very well. I will see you then. Oh, and Phoebe...'

'Yes Mr. Collins?'

'Please remember to call me Jonah.'

'Yes Mr. C... Jonah, argh sorry! I will try.'

'Thank you, Phoebe. I look forward to seeing you tonight.'

I just needed to find a cover story to tell Mum.

Soon after a meagre brunch, being all that I could stomach, Denise called me. 'Hey Phoebs. How are ya?'

I wasn't sure if it was a good idea to spill the beans about Mr. Collins to Denise yet, so I tried to contain the enthusiasm in my own voice. 'Hi Denise. I'm great. How 'bout you?'

'Oh my God babe—I am just so over the moon, and I can't wait for tonight. Guess who will be there?'

Oh crap! I had completely forgotten about Justine's party! 'I can't guess, sorry Denise.'

'Curtis and Nick—those guys from the bus on Thursday morning! Curtis rang me just then and when I told him about the party, he was like, "Well I would love to be your plus one if you'll have me."

And I said that would be fab and then he asked if Nick could come because he figured Nick would love to see you there.'

How was I going to get out of this party? 'That's great Denise. Sounds like Curtis really likes you.' Then I knew… 'The problem is babe, I have to go and stay at Dad's tonight, so I can't make it. Please send my apologies to Justine and the others.'

'Oh man that really sucks. I was so looking forward to seeing you there and it will be such a fun night. I hear Justine got a frozen daiquiri machine and several kegs of beer and cider.'

A pang of guilt rushed over me, and I swore to myself I would not lie to Denise again. 'I promise to make the next one. And we can meet up next week, so you can fill me in on all the gory details.'

'Ok hun, I better go and start planning what to wear tonight. Have fun at your dad's.' The slight tone of sarcasm in her voice was not lost on me, but I could not let this dampen my spirits.

I had my cover-story sorted, so it was time to start planning my own wardrobe. To be a convincing cover, I needed to look the part and I didn't think Mr. Collins would mind seeing me in party attire. I decided on the classic 'little black dress' to appeal to his sense of class. The one I chose was relatively conservative; I figured this would be suggestive without being overtly explicit. *What about underwear?* Because Mr. Collins only just took my virginity, I had very little lingerie to speak of. I only had two matching sets that were slightly sexy, one was black lace and the other white lace. Everything else I owned was cotton. I decided to go with black cotton to maintain a sense of innocence. I kept the makeup minimal, which was my usual style, even for parties. I left the full glamour look to the likes of Denise and Justine.

຺ꖥꙅ

I was feeling too excited and nervous about visiting Mr. Collins to eat much, so I decided to skip dinner and catch public transport straight there. His house was on the other side of town, so I needed a couple of connecting buses, but I didn't mind because it filled in the time; plus, it gave me a chance to zone out with my thoughts.

From outward appearances, his home was a modest sized townhouse of relatively modern design. I buzzed the intercom on the gate and was promptly greeted by the crackly voice of Mr. Collins, somewhat distorted by the speaker box. 'Hello Phoebe. The gate and door are both unlocked. Please come in.'

The gate clicked and locked behind me after I stepped through and I continued up the paved walkway, noticing a few potted herbs and cottage style flowers in the courtyard. When I walked inside the house, my impressions of it were instantly

18

changed. For one thing, the interior seemed more spacious than the façade led me to believe possible. The whole ground floor was a large open-plan living area with high ceilings covered in downlights, large windows, and minimal furniture. Several modern art pieces decorated the walls, each showcased by their own spotlights, making the whole space feel like an art gallery.

He was sitting stiffly upright on the leather couch when I entered. It occurred to me then that I had never seen this man slouch. I wondered if he even knew how to relax.

'Please join me for a drink Phoebe.' He gestured for me to sit, placing one hand on the seat beside him. It was then that I noticed the open bottle of merlot accompanied by two glasses on the coffee table. As soon as I sat down, he turned towards me, grabbed my arms with incredible force, and pulled me in close for a kiss.

Just like that, we forgot the wine.

After we emerged from our frenzy, Mr. Collins swept up the mess of broken glass as he asked, 'I do not know about you, but I am famished. Have you eaten?'

'I have barely touched any food today, so wouldn't mind a bite to eat.' I confessed.

'Do you like fish?' he inquired.

'Yes, very much, thank you.'

He smiled. 'Very well, I shall prepare some *filet de*

Poisson with a *gribiche* salad.'

'Sounds complicated. What's *Poisson*?' I asked.

'*Poisson* is the French word for fish and the meal is quite simple to prepare. Please make yourself at home and enjoy some wine while you wait.'

Still naked, I sipped on some wine with the remaining, unbroken glass, and watched him with curiosity as he busied himself in the kitchen. Mr. Collins, however, had dressed properly before he started cooking. The meal he was making seemed to involve tossing some salad greens together with boiled eggs and wholegrain mustard, which he served atop some grilled fish. It came together very quickly, so I threw my dress back on, and joined him at the breakfast bar since there was no proper dining table. He sat so close to me that our legs were touching, making it hard to focus entirely on the food. Engaging in some small talk during the meal, it occurred to me that Mr. Collins was finally at ease, (although still not slouching), which allowed me to see a new side of him.

We retired to the bedroom after dinner, then he drove me home in his Mercedes at some pre-dawn hour of morning.

Chapter Three

Diary extract dated Tuesday 17ᵗʰ April 2001

'Well, it is your turn again meh lady'

His silly accent made me laugh, distracting me such that I tripped over a ledge. He was quick to respond, catching me before I fell, and we were both caught in a momentary locked gaze before he released my arm.

The rest of Easter passed by in a bit of a haze, my attention only half-focused on my time with Dad while my mind wondered back to thoughts of Mr. Collins. The one conversation that I clearly remembered was book focused and it was had over a cup of tea in the comfort of the old leather armchairs in his library.

'Read any good books lately?' he asked.

This was a quip as much as it was an actual question that one of us always used to start our favourite discussion.

'I just finished *Chocolat* by Joanne Harris.' I told him.

'I'm not familiar with that one. What's it about?'

I paused to reflect carefully because I knew Dad would want something deeper than a simple plot summary. 'It's about love, temptation, sensual awakenings, and breaking the rules. It also features a bit of magic.'

'That is impressively insightful Phoebe. Your literary analysis skills have come a long way. I think I'm going to have to give it a read myself now.'

I felt a warm glow of pride then because I knew Dad was not the sort to dish out compliments lightly.

'What about yourself, Dad? What was the last thing you read?'

'I have just finished reading a book called *Stardust* by Neil Gaiman.'

I was familiar with the author, but not the title. 'Interesting title. What's it about?'

'Well, it has a 19th Century English setting to start with, but it steps into a fantastic world filled with magic. The story is essentially about the protagonist's coming of age. It's also about love, courage, following your dreams, and power struggles.'

'Sounds good.'

ଛଠଔ

Denise rang me on Sunday night with the exciting

news about Curtis. 'It happened Phoebs! Curtis and I made out last night! And he wants to keep seeing me.'

It was good to hear Denise so happy, especially when I was also feeling rapturous. It was just a pity I still wasn't sure if I could tell anyone yet. 'That's awesome hun! So now I'm dying to know, how far did you guys go?' I knew that Denise wasn't a virgin anymore, she had slept with a couple of guys before, but those guys didn't stick around for long and I suspected that had something to do with how soon she jumped into bed with them. For her sake I was really hoping that she was taking things slower with Curtis.

'Only to second base. He seems like a real gentleman, you know.'

Honestly, I didn't know. My first impression of the guy was that of an egotist, but if he made Denise happy, and wasn't pushing her into anything too quickly, I would cut him some slack. 'That is good news. I hope things work out for you this time. I'm sick of guys that treat you like dirt.'

'Nick asked after you, by the way. He said your absence surprised him, and he looked quite disappointed.'

I rolled my eyes. 'Do you think he likes me?' I was mostly asking to go along with the conversation, although I was a little curious.

'I don't think it could be any more obvious babe.

He was definitely jonesing for you.'

I'll admit to feeling flattered. 'Hmm, perhaps we could go on a double date sometime soon.' I wasn't all that serious about the idea of dating him, but I knew Denise loved the concept of double dating, so the suggestion was for her benefit.

'Oh my God—that is the best idea ever! Let's do it. I'll ring Curtis and put the idea to him.'

So that's how we ended up playing mini golf on Tuesday.

The golf course was next to the beach and attached to a games arcade and small amusement park. It was a very popular destination in the summer, but we had the course pretty much to ourselves thanks to the cooler weather. I had opted for neat dress pants, polo shirt, and a sports jacket, clothing well-suited to golf and the weather. Denise, however, was wearing her netball skirt and a low-cut V-neck designer jumper. It amazed me that she wasn't shivering from the cold. When the guys arrived, Denise ran straight into Curtis' arms and they kissed, leaving Nick and me standing in awkward silence for a moment.

He shrugged and smiled at me. 'Hi. Phoebe, isn't it?'

'Yes, that's right. And you're Nick?' Of course, I knew, but sometimes it's fun to play along with the pantomime.

Nick had dressed in plain black track pants, a simple t-shirt, and woollen jacket, giving the overall impression that he preferred comfortable and practical clothing over anything especially fashionable. Curtis was also casually dressed, but in a designer tracksuit that looked tailored to fit. It made him look like a professional athlete.

When the lovebirds finally came up for some air, Curtis addressed the group, 'All right ladies, Nick. Let's get our game on. I must warn you, though, I'm a mini-golf master. Please don't feel that you have to keep up with me!'

I rolled my eyes at this, something that only Nick was witness to, and this made him laugh as we walked on up to the counter to collect our equipment.

When we reached the first hole Nick gestured for me to start. 'Ladies first.'

I played the first few holes well, coming under par each time, and this seemed to impress Nick. Denise missed hitting the ball the first time, so predictably, Curtis stepped up to hold her as he guided her arms through the correct method for swinging the club. Her game improved soon after this, although her score was still much higher than anyone else's. Curtis meanwhile proved that his words were no mere bluff, scoring better than any of us. On the fourth hole, Nick started up a conversation with me. 'Tell me about yourself, Phoebe. What do you enjoy? What are your dreams for the future?'

So, I told him about my love of books and my

dream to study literature at university. 'I haven't really decided if I want to be a writer, an editor, or a publisher, but I know that I want to work with books.'

'It's good that you have some vision at least.'

I paused to let him take his shot. When he had finished, he bent over to pick up the ball from the hole and I couldn't help but notice how shapely his backside was. *Oh God! What was I thinking?* 'What about yourself, Nick?'

'I love acting. It is my dream to get into NIDA one day. That's where most big-name Australian actors kick-start their careers.'

'It seems that you not only have vision, but ambition.'

'Hmm, maybe a little, but nothing like Curtis here. He is determined to be a lawyer and I know he will be damn good at it. He is a straight-A student and does not settle for less than perfect.'

'Yes, I can see that.'

I noticed that Curtis was staring fixedly at Denise's backside with a big grin on his face. She was bending over to pick up her ball and her black lace panties were clearly visible from beneath her skirt. Nick brought my attention back to our conversation as we moved on to the next hole. This was when I tripped.

Denise jumped forward to voice her concern, 'Oh my God are you ok hun?'

Smiling at Nick, who was still holding me, I replied, 'Yes, I'm fine. Nick came to my rescue just in time.'

He seemed very pleased at this acknowledgement and become even more attentive to me for the remainder of the game.

Afterwards, we all grabbed a bite to eat at a sushi bar before heading home. Nick insisted on paying for my share of the meal, so Curtis followed suit and covered Denise. Nick then asked how I was planning to get home, offering to give me a lift if I needed one. I told him that Denise was driving me but thanked him for the offer. He seemed a little cut by this, so I promised to catch up with him again soon.

Chapter Four

I feel something deeper and more substantial than the mere lust that had first defined our relationship. Am I falling for Mr. Collins? Is the feeling mutual?

Shortly after Mum left for work in the morning, I was looking at my phone and thinking about calling Mr. Collins when I heard the door. I thought it was a bit early for door knockers, so I answered wondering if Mum had left her keys inside again. It wasn't Mum though.

Mr. Collins was there in the flesh. I was a little surprised and then embarrassment hit when I remembered I was still in my pyjamas. Blushing I said, 'Um, Hi Jonah.'

'Hi Phoebe. Please forgive the intrusion, but I see that your mother has left, and it has been a few days since I heard from you, so I wanted to check that everything is okay... May I come in?'

'Um, yes, of course. Sorry.'

As soon as I had closed the door, he embraced me, holding me tight. His essence surrounded me entirely, so I melted into his arms and rested my head against his chest. He lifted my chin up to face him and kissed me deeply.

I was suddenly aware of movement, then realised he was carrying me across the family room towards the hallway. 'Which room is yours, Phoebe?'

I barely had access to the higher functioning parts of my brain at this point, so it was just as well I was able to answer instinctively. 'First on the left.'

We were through my bedroom door in no time, and he gently placed me on the bed. He did not rush to undress me, but rather he took his time kissing and caressing me with his large, strong hands. He spent some time kissing my neck and gently tugging at my earlobes with his teeth before returning to my lips. This was my moment of realisation.

He stood up to undress, giving me the opportunity to take in the whole sight of his naked body at once. Like his arms, his chest was well toned and only slightly hairy, with a trail that led my eyes down to his waist and beyond. He returned and slowly removed my pyjamas, covering every part of my body with kisses as he went. Then he was inside me and the familiar passion returned.

ഇറ

I awoke from my sleep and found that I was still in his arms, with my head on his chest. We must have collapsed from exhaustion after spending what felt like hours. Mr. Collins was still sleeping, and I was not inclined to disturb him, so I just propped my head against my hand and watched him for a while. He looked so peaceful. Then, almost without thought, I moved my hand to gently stroke his hair, prompting him to stir from his slumber.

He was still groggy. 'Mm, you are wonderful Phoebe. I must have drifted off to sleep.' He yawned. 'What is the time?'

I had no idea, so I turned to check my clock and gasped. 'It's three in the afternoon.'

He sat upright; eyes wide. 'Gosh, really? What time does your mother get home?'

'Relax, it's ok, she doesn't get home until five thirty at the earliest.'

He was starting to get dressed at this point, although I was still naked beneath the quilt. 'That is a relief, although I really must get going soon. I have things to attend to at home.' Kissing me briefly on the forehead, he added, 'Thank you for today, Phoebe.'

I had grown extremely fond of the way he spoke my name in private. When he had dressed, he sat on the edge of my bed, lifted some of my long hair aside, and kissed me fervently. 'I am free tomorrow. Will you visit me?'

'Yes, I would love to.... Jonah?'

'Yes Phoebe?'

'I've been meaning to ask you something.'

He sat back on my bed. 'Then ask.'

'Is it okay if I tell Denise about us?'

He deliberated a while before responding. 'I do not think that would be wise. We need to keep this a secret for the time being, at least until you have finished school. Telling anyone could jeopardise things for us.'

'Okay, I think I understand.'

Then we kissed one last time before he left.

Chapter Five

I can really feel a bond forming between us. There is nothing quite like connecting through common music tastes.

When I sensed him leaning in to kiss me, my own reservations about Jonah paralysed me.

That's when we heard the screams.

The rest of the week passed by in a flash. I spent both Thursday and Friday at Jonah's house, and I was finally getting used to his first name. Both days unfolded in much the same way as Wednesday, although we did at least manage lunch on these occasions.

Saturday night was party night and this time I had a promise to keep. I knew that Nick was going to be there, which got me thinking. I liked Nick, there was no point denying it. *But if something happened between us, would I be cheating on Jonah?* I didn't know if we were in an exclusive relationship and I was not prepared to sabotage what we had, so I decided that I would keep Nick in the friend zone for the time being.

I didn't need to think too hard about what to wear this time because Denise insisted on picking out a new dress for me at the shops during the day. She seemed more excited for me than I was. I guess she had strong hopes for Nick and me. So, as a result, I rocked up in a red halter-neck dress that left my shoulders and lower legs bare, and—because I got ready at Denise's house—more makeup than I was comfortable with.

Curtis and Nick were already there when we arrived and there was no hiding in that outfit. I hadn't intended to make much of an entrance, but when I walked in, I turned most of the heads of those attendants with a Y-chromosome and even some without. I could see Nick approaching me, but then Justine grabbed me.

The girls from school squealed at the sight of me, pulling me in for an obligatory round of hugs and gossip, before showing me to the drinks bar. I had always found Justine's catering beyond generous, but this was something else. There was a fully stocked cocktail bar, complete with recipes and several blenders. I made myself something called a Sidecar and then settled into the lounge area with the girls. The stereo was pumping out plenty of my favourite R&B tracks, including Aaliyah, Destiny's Child, and J. Lo.

This was when Nick caught up with me. 'There you are. I hope you aren't trying to hide from me.'

'Hi Nick. Sorry, Justine abducted me. You'd think it'd been years, not a little over a week since we saw each other last.' I grinned at Justine, and she made a show of poking out her tongue.

Nick laughed, then looking at my drink, he continued, 'It's all good. That drink looks a little lethal. What's in it?'

'Mostly Cognac and Cointreau,' I told him.

He grinned. 'I'm not wrong then.' Holding up his drink he added, 'I think I'll stick with beer for now.'

I laughed. 'I promise I'll take my time drinking it.'

Eyeing me intently, he asked, 'So, you handled that golf club pretty well. Do you play any other sports?'

'Yes actually, I play netball. What about you?'

'Awesome. I play tennis and squash for fun, not competitively. Have you been playing long?'

'Since I was five. I'm in the A-grade team at school. We practise three times a week and compete most weekends during the school term.'

'I'd love to see you play sometime,' he hinted.

Britney's *Oops!... I did It Again* came on, so Denise grabbed me and pulled me onto the dancefloor. This had become a favourite for the girls to dance to. The guys weren't shy in joining us either. Not wanting to lead him on, I tried not to get too close to Nick. Denise and Curtis disappeared as soon as the song finished, but I decided to stay on with the other girls and so did Nick. *Damn that man had some good moves!*

When I retired to the bar for a refill and breather, Nick followed. This time I kept it simple and just made a vodka raspberry mix and Nick grabbed another beer. Denise was right: it was obvious that he liked me, so I maintained a respectful distance when we sat down to talk.

The music had shifted into a more electronic mode and *Lady (Hear Me Tonight)* by Modjo was playing. 'Oh wow, I love this song!' Nick exclaimed. 'Pity I'm too bushed to dance right now.'

'Oh my God—Yes. I love it too!' I told him.

He smiled at me. 'Ah, so you like electronica too then, not just R&B and Pop?'

'For sure!'

Shifting a little closer, Nick continued, 'Ok, let me try you with a few songs—tell me what you think alright?'

'Alright' I agreed.

'What about *One More Time* by Daft Punk?'

'Love it! Ok, let me try you with one. What do you think of *American Dream* by Jakatta?'

He put his arm on my shoulder in response. 'Oh man that one's awesome. *Hey Boy Hey Girl* by the Chemical Brothers?'

'Eh, it's ok. What about *Who the Hell Are You?* by Madison Avenue?'

To my surprise, he scowled a little. 'Not a favourite, gotta say. Alright—ATB's *9pm 'til I Come*?'

I couldn't contain my excitement as a replied, '*Yes!* Totally! Faithless—*God is a DJ*?'

'Absolutely! I love Faithless, especially *Insomnia*.' He started to lean in, and I sensed his desire to kiss me.

That was when we heard the screams and a loud crashing sound outside followed by Justine shouting, '*Someone, call an ambulance!*'

We ran outside to see what the commotion was. Curtis was lying unconscious bleeding from his head, with the weapon, a smashed beer bottle, next to him. Denise was crying uncontrollably at his side, trying to wake him and one of the guys nearby moved in to start first aid. I could barely move; I was so shocked by the scene.

Nick stepped up to ask the question that was certainly on my mind. 'What the hell happened here?'

A very nervous Justine came forward, sobbing in between words, 'It was... gate-crashers! They... busted through... the side... entrance. Started... a fight... then... ran off.'

Nick was angry. 'Holy shit man! The cops had better be called too!'

Justine was beside herself. 'But... the... booze.

Most… of… us… are under… age.'

'*Fuck the booze, Justine! This is my friend's life at risk here. Those bastards have got to pay!*'

Seeing Nick lose his temper snapped me out of my daze, so I moved up to comfort him with a hug, finding my words. 'He has a point, Justine. Besides, I'm sure the paramedics will call the police anyway, so you better tell anyone that was not a witness to go home, then clear away as much of the alcohol as you can.'

She seemed to understand because she calmed down a little and started running about telling people what to do.

Nick held me close, and I could feel him shaking. 'Thank you, Phoebe.'

We could hear the ambulance arrive, so we cleared a path for them to access Curtis. The police were close behind and when they entered, they started taking witness statements.

A female officer approached us. 'Can I please see your IDs?'

We both retrieved our wallets and showed her. I could see on Nick's licence that he was recently eighteen.

The woman grabbed her pen and notepad and noted our names. 'Did either of you witness the fight?'

Nick replied that he had not, and I shook my head.

'You are going to have to speak up miss,' the

officer insisted.

'No, sorry. I didn't see anything until we heard the screams. When we came outside, Curtis was already down, and the gate-crashers had fled.'

'So, you both know the victim?' she asked.

We replied 'Yes' in unison.

'What are your relationships to him?'

Nick took a deep breath. 'He is my best mate. Phoebe knows him through me.'

'Can you please provide me with his parents' contact details?'

Nick retrieved his mobile phone and looked up a number for her.

She jotted down the details. 'Thank you. Now, have either of you supplied alcohol to minors here tonight?'

We both gave her a resounding 'No.'

I told her, 'Justine is the hostess. She will know where the alcohol came from.'

'That will be all. Thank you.' She left us to join her fellow officers.

Nick found out which hospital they were taking Curtis to, then called a taxi. 'I'm going to the hospital. Will you come with me Phoebe?'

'Of course. I don't want to leave you alone in this state. And I'm sure Denise will need some comforting too.'

I found Denise inside with a male police officer, still giving her statement. When she had finished, the officer asked for her parent's phone number. 'Now I'm sorry miss, but I am going to have to call your parents to pick you up because you're a minor and you've been drinking.'

Protesting got her nowhere and she broke down crying again.

I ran up to embrace her. 'Is this really necessary?' I asked the officer. 'I'm her best friend and I'm eighteen. Can't I just take her home in a taxi?'

'Sorry miss, but I have a duty of care to ensure she reaches her parents safely. Now please excuse me while I make this call.'

He stepped aside and rang Denise's folks.

Her Mum, Dana, arrived promptly, heaving a sigh when she discovered that her daughter had not incurred any injuries. Taking Denise from me into her own arms, she glanced at me. 'Hi Phoebe. What happened here?'

I told her about the fight and explained that Curtis had gone to hospital. Denise had told her mum about her relationship with Curtis, so Dana understood her daughter's feelings.

'Well, we better get along to the hospital then, hadn't we?' she said, smiling warmly.

Nick, who had been standing next to me the whole time, made a fake coughing sound.

I felt so rude. 'Oh right, sorry. Dana, this is Nick, Curtis' best friend.'

'Hi Nick. Would you like a lift to the hospital too?'

Dana asked.

Nick shook his head. 'Thanks, but I called a taxi.'

'Someone else can take it when it arrives. Come on.'

₧₨

When we arrived at the waiting room in the Emergency Department, Nick gestured towards a seated couple. 'Curtis' parents, Tony and Angela.'

So, we approached them. Recognising Nick, they stood up to greet us. Nick made all the introductions. They seemed a little surprised when he introduced Denise as Curtis' girlfriend.

'Any news on his condition?' Nick asked.

'Nothing yet, I'm afraid,' replied Tony.

We all sat quietly waiting in anticipation. Tony and Nick stood up every time a doctor walked into the waiting room, their shoulders sagging when the doctor walked straight past. During this time, I sat in between Nick and Denise. Dana was still holding Denise, so I was able to focus on comforting Nick.

Eventually, after about three hours, a doctor approached us. We all stood to attention this time. 'Curtis is conscious and in a stable condition.'

We all breathed out a sigh of relief.

The doctor continued, 'He has a pretty nasty cut above his right eye that will take some time to heal and likely leave a permanent scar, but there are no signs of brain damage or other internal injuries. He is clearly concussed though, so we want to keep him in for observation a little longer.'

'Can we see him?' Tony asked.

'Yes, but only two at a time. Please keep it brief and light.'

We waited until everyone else had seen him, then Nick and I entered the emergency bay, arms linked. Curtis had a large bandage wrapped around his forehead, but he was sitting up and had his eyes open.

Nick greeted him with a fist bump. 'Hey man. You gave us a scare. How ya feeling?'

'Hey Nick, Hi Phoebe. My head's pounding and I keep feeling like I'm gonna puke, but I'm in one piece, so it can't be all bad. The doctors tell me my head's okay, too.'

I smiled. 'That's a relief. You should be back to conquering mini golf courses all over the world in no time.'

Curtis laughed, then started vomiting. A nurse came over to help him, reassuring us that this was completely normal for concussion and nothing to worry about. 'It is probably time to let him get some rest, though.'

We headed back out to the waiting room. Tony and Angela had already left by this stage, so we just reconvened with Denise and Dana. Dana gave Nick a lift home, then took us back to her home where I had planned to crash after the party.

Sleep was not easily had that night. Denise needed help settling after the shock she suffered, and I had a lot of feelings of my own to process. *My feelings for Jonah were very strong, so why couldn't I get Nick out of my mind?*

Chapter Six

He dropped the phone to the floor; his face was ashen when he turned to look at me. As though suddenly registering he was still naked, he rushed to put his robe on then gave me my own clothes. 'You must dress quickly and be gone from here. You cannot be alone with me anymore.'

I should mention something of the party aftermath before moving on. Denise recovered from her shock by the end of the weekend, although she was not her usual bubbly self until a few days later. Both Dana and my mum were very understanding about our need to skip church that Sunday; so, I spent some quality time with Denise.

The hospital discharged Curtis late Sunday afternoon on the condition that he rest up at home for several days. Nick was very attentive to his mate's welfare, refusing to let him spend the rest of the week unsupervised while Tony and Angela were busy at work. He didn't forget me either, calling practically every night that week to see how I was and chat for a bit. Upon hanging up from one such call, I remember thinking how easily we carried our conversations—although we never broached the topic of our almost kiss, nor was anything outside of normal friendship boundaries. I started to wonder if Nick wanted anything more.

Justine's parents absolutely flipped when they needed to return from their vacation early because the police called them. As a result, they grounded her until her eighteenth birthday in November. This came as a blow to a lot of my friends who had always considered Justine's house to be 'party central.'

৪১৫

Much of what occupied my time that week was English: Jonah by day, homework by night. He even helped me with my studies a little during the days I spent with him. Friday afternoon was when the distressing news came. I had curled up comfortably beneath the quilt on Jonah's bed, listening to him read the poetry of John Donne, when the phone on his bedside table rang. This was the call that changed everything, the one that prompted him to end our relationship.

Bolting upright I asked, 'Why? What's going on Jonah? Why can't I be with you?' Tears welled in my eyes. *What was that phone call about, why the urgency?*

Remembering that I was not privy to his phone conversation, he dropped back on the bed and addressed me mournfully, 'Oh gosh, Phoebe, I am so sorry. The universe dealt me such a blow that I almost forgot my manners. The reason we can no longer be together is that I am your teacher once again.'

I felt as though my heart rested precariously on a corroding precipice. My voice was stammering. 'B-but why... how?'

'St. Mark's College have rescinded my employment offer, but they were able to negotiate my return to St. Teresa's College on my behalf because no one has replaced me yet. I cannot wait for other teaching positions, so I must accept the reinstatement.'

There it went, that last piece of rock supporting my heart fell away, leaving it to plummet into the icy cold waters below. I collapsed against his chest and began to cry. He said nothing, simply holding me close, letting me come to terms with my loss.

When I no longer felt able to weep, due to exhaustion more than anything else, I put my clothing back on in complete silence. The air in the room was so tense that, if struck, it would sound as guitar strings in a minor key. When I made for the door Jonah stopped me for one last embrace. I desperately wanted to kiss him, sensing that he wanted this too.

He sighed. 'We must be content with this for now. It has been a joy to spend these last two weeks consummating an affection for you that has grown over the years, but I need to exercise restraint again.'

I stepped back out into the cold, cruel world and floundered home.

Chapter Seven
Diary extract dated Monday 30ᵗʰ April 2001

Today's English lesson is the worst ever! Seeing Mr. Collins stirs up so many emotions for me that I am unable to focus on my studies at all. This compounded with the fact that he refuses to make eye contact with me and the only time he spoke my name was for the roll call in home group. Restraint is one thing, but why does he have to ignore me?

I shut myself away that weekend, feigning illness to all who tried to coax me out. Knowing that I would have to return to school and face reality on Monday, I indulge my broken heart in the meantime. I wrote a lot of words of anguish in my diary on those days, including a sonnet.

If Our Love is a Game
A Sonnet by Phoebe Braddock

If our love is a game, we play it with fire
First you kindle the spark,
Then set my heart at the pyre
Watch as it burns, then leave when it's dark

If our love is a game, you play me to win
First, we race to the top,
Then surrender in sin
You leave me wanting for more just as you stop

If our love is a game, you are playing no more
First you get what you want,
Then you stop keeping score
Why didn't we play with our pieces upfront?

The rules of this game are far too complex
Perhaps I'm too young to engage with your sex

౮౦౧౪

When I saw Denise on the bus Monday morning, I was not very talkative, despite her best efforts.

She looked at me with a worried expression. 'What's wrong, Phoebs?'

Resting my head back against the seat, I closed my eyes. 'I'm still not feeling well.'

The sight of Mr. Collins in home group came as a surprise to the rest of the girls, but it had an entirely different effect on me. It took all my willpower to stay seated and not betray my feelings. I couldn't keep my eyes off him though, and I kept waiting for his gaze to meet mine, but it never did.

The first lesson of the day was double English, something I used to consider an ideal way to start the school week, but this time I dreaded it. It really was the worst English lesson ever.

We spent the first half on shared group reading of the new book we had just started, *Like Water for Chocolate* by Laura Esquivel. I had spent some time during the school break reading ahead with this, so it hardly mattered that I wasn't keeping up. For the remainder of the lesson, Mr. Collins instructed us to do some quiet study, which meant personal reading and note taking. I just pretended to read while I let my thoughts wander and wrote in my diary. I couldn't help but compare my feelings of longing to those felt by Tita, (the book's protagonist), for Pedro, her forbidden lover.

༄༅

Given the way Mr. Collins was behaving, I decided to skip netball practice that afternoon, asking Denise to send my apologies. When I walked out of the school gate, I found Nick waiting for me.

'Hello miss Phoebe Braddock. *How do you do*?' His playful, melodramatic tone made me smile for the first time that day.

'I'm not feeling a hundred percent, to be honest.'

His expression changed to one of genuine concern. 'That's no good. I hope it's nothing serious.'

'I'm sure it'll pass soon enough. I just need rest.'

'Well in that case, I'll drive you home and I won't accept any protests.'

I conceded, 'You are too kind, Mr. Willoughby.'

Nick's car impressed me; a stunning electric blue coloured Honda Civic that was only a few years old. I relaxed into the cosy upholstery. Once the engine was running, my attention was drawn to the music coming through the stereo. It wasn't loud, thankfully, but it was good, so I questioned Nick, 'What CD have you got playing?'

He pulled into traffic before replying, 'It's a Ministry of Sound compilation. You like it?'

'Yes, very much.'

Eyes still on the road, he grinned somewhat demurely. 'I will have to keep that in mind.'

We didn't talk for the rest of the drive, which was fine because it allowed me to zone out and enjoy the music. I loved the fact that we could enjoy each other's company without feeling compelled to fill the time with words.

When we pulled into my driveway, I turned to him. 'Thanks for the lift.'

He smiled. 'Not a problem. I live around the corner anyway. Take care and get well soon.'

'Will do.' After getting out of the car, I waved goodbye. Mum was outside, observing the nature of my arrival, which caught me a little off-guard since I wasn't used to seeing her home so early. 'Was that a young man I saw at the wheel of that flashy looking car?'

'Um, hi Mum. Yes, that's my friend Nick. Why are you home so early?'

'Nick, hmm?' she asked in a half teasing, half apprehensive manner.

Oh boy, I had hoped Mum would let up on the whole dating-boys-thing by the time I turned eighteen. 'He is still just a friend Mum. I met him through Denise. He goes to St. Mark's and lives nearby, so he offered to drive me home. He is a proper gentleman, so you don't need to worry.'

'I'd like to be the judge of that.' Thankfully, she left it there and changed the subject. 'My afternoon clients cancelled, so I decided to come home early for you. I figured you could use some pampering after last weekend, and we haven't had much quality time lately.' Mum was a clinical psychiatrist, a job she was very good at and seemed to enjoy immensely. Even when she wasn't at work, she was often reading books and journals on the subject which would excite her.

'Sounds good. Thanks Mum.'

She wasn't kidding about the pampering either. First, she prepared a DIY sushi platter for our dinner. I loved eating Japanese food this way because it meant that we could customise our fillings. Plus, it was fun to assemble our own nori rolls. She then gave me a facial and a manicure while playing some relaxing new-age music in the background. I felt like I was in a real beauty spa! This was exactly what I needed to get my mind off Mr. Collins, so by the end of the night I was feeling a lot better and able to sleep soundly.

Chapter Eight

Diary extract dated Sunday 6th May 2001

"Do you have any emotional attachments Phoebe?'

Finally! I thought. 'You mean like a boyfriend? No. I'm single.'

He grinned as he replied, 'Good to know.'

He began to run his finger along my arm, 'You look... very nice tonight... my dear.'

I inhaled deeply at the sensation that his touch sent through my body. 'Thanks,' was all I could manage.

B y the weekend, things were finally settling into some form of normality. I had not forgotten about Mr. Collins by any means; I simply found it easier to put my mind to other tasks, and people.

Denise extended an invitation from Curtis to attend his birthday party on Saturday night. She was beside herself with excitement for this event and called on me for help picking out a gift for him as well as a new outfit. 'So, Nick still hasn't made his move huh?' she queried while picking a few different tops off the rack.

I sighed, 'Alas no. I fear that he just isn't all that into me.'

'That can't be true, hun! I have seen the way he looks at you. He just needs some encouragement.' She grabbed a few pairs of jeans then made for the change room. Just before disappearing into a cubicle, she added, 'Why don't you find an irresistible outfit of your own?'

I decided that was worth a shot and went with an Aaliyah inspired outfit, a black crop-top with mesh sleeves and black satin cargo pants. When I stepped out of the change room to show Denise, she exhaled sharply. 'Damn girl, you look hot!'

We arrived early so that Denise could get in a bit of quality time with Curtis before most of the guests arrived.

Curtis answered the door. 'Hi ladies. Come in.'

Denise burst into the house, flinging her arms around him. 'Happy birthday babe!' She locked him in a kiss for several minutes.

Nick came along the hall, his face lighting up when he saw me, and he didn't even try to hide the way his eyes took in my attire. 'Hi Phoebe. I'm so glad you came. Are you feeling better?'

'Yes much, thanks Nick.'

'Let's give those two a moment. Come with me.' He grabbed my hand and started leading me through the house, an enormous federation style home. 'Do you like video games?' he asked.

We had reached the living area by this time. 'Um, I don't know. I haven't really played many.'

He sat me down on the couch next to him and handed me a controller. 'This is what I got Curtis for his birthday. It's pretty fun.' He showed me the case for a PlayStation 2 game called *Midnight Club: Street Racing*. 'Here let me show you.' He talked me through what each button did, then we had a race. I was lousy at steering my car, but it was a lot of fun.

When Denise and Curtis returned, I offered up my controller to Curtis and greeted him properly, 'Hey Curtis, Happy birthday!'

'Thanks, Phoebs.' He took the controller and played one more round with Nick before turning off the console and getting the music cranked.

As more guests arrived, Curtis and Nick introduced me to their friends. Of the guys I could remember, there was Chad who seemed quite aloof at first, but warmed up after a few drinks; Tyler and Drew, who were both very polite and amiable all night; Justin who seemed nice, but didn't stick around for much conversation; Shane had a pretty blonde girl hanging off his arm all night and spent most of his time making out with her; and Ben, who was a little too friendly for my liking, but seemed harmless enough, especially when distracted by some of my own school friends.

Nick and I spent a lot of time dancing, but when we both tired of this, we found a quiet room to relax in.

Before joining me on the couch, Nick observed, 'This room is almost too quiet. Some radio ought to help.' He tuned into a dance music station but kept the volume to a background level. 'Perfect.' He said as he sat down close beside me.

I smiled, then added, 'Yes, a very good choice of music.'

He cocked an eyebrow at that, then clarified, 'I wasn't just referring to the music.'

'Oh?' I prompted.

At that moment, a drunk couple chose to interrupt the mood as they stumbled through on their way to the bedrooms. When the peace returned, Nick asked if I was dating anyone, then complimented me on my attire.

His face was extremely close to mine at this stage, but his gaze was downcast. When he finally looked up into my eyes, we remained transfixed looking at each other for an infinite measure of time. Suddenly, he stood up, 'I'm going to get us something to drink.'

What the actual hell? Why didn't he just kiss me? Was

he waiting for me to make a move? I wasn't sure if I had that sort of courage. *What if I was reading him completely wrong?*

He returned with a couple of premixed drinks. 'I hope this is okay?' he inquired, handing me a vodka–raspberry. 'I have memories of you mixing your own vodka drinks at Justine's party.'

'Yes, this is good. Thank you.' I smiled, trying to hide my disappointment.

His own drink was a Canadian Club with cola. When he sat down, we returned to more mundane conversation for a few hours. It was still nice to be able to talk so freely with him.

After a while I started to grow tired. Nick must have seen that I was struggling to keep my eyelids open when he suggested, 'Looks like I need to tuck you into bed for the night.'

I yawned, then replied, 'Oh God, sorry. Yes, I think bed is exactly what I need.'

At this, he picked me up and carried me to a spare room where he gently placed me on the bed and removed my shoes. He started to make for the door, but I stopped him, 'Please stay with me, Nick.'

I heard his intake of breath. Then he turned off the light and sat on the bed to remove his own shoes. When he lay down on his back, I curled up into his arms with my head on his chest and drifted off to sleep.

৪৩

When I awoke in the morning, Nick was already up and cleaning with the others. I offered to help, but they had essentially finished by the time I joined them. Denise needed to get going, so when she offered me a lift home, I accepted. I really needed to talk to her, besides which, we had netball later that afternoon. When she kissed Curtis goodbye, Nick hugged me briefly. 'See you again soon, Phoebe.'

'Yes.' I hoped my succinct reply didn't betray my frustration.

Once we were in the car, Denise asked, 'Sooo, what happened with Nick?'

'Not much I'm afraid.' I told her what transpired between us.

Denise sounded astonished. 'What the hell is wrong with him? Is he blind?'

'I don't know hun. I think he just wants to be friends.'

'But why would he ask if you're single?'

She had a point. I just sighed and changed the subject.

Chapter Nine

'This abstinence simply will not do anymore. I cannot bear to see you or hear your voice without having all of you.'

Nick was waiting for me after school on Tuesday, this time with Curtis, who must have known Denise would be with me. The four of us got a drink at the local café before parting ways. This time I saw Denise grab a ride with Curtis, who drove a shiny, silver, convertible Mazda. When she got into the car, several other girls from our school crowded around to admire the vehicle (and its driver).

Nick gave me another lift. 'I'm more than happy to drive you home every afternoon, especially since I live so close.'

'That's so kind, thanks, but I normally have netball practice until late on Mondays, Wednesdays, and Fridays. I wouldn't expect you to wait around on those nights.'

He sighed. 'Yeah, I probably shouldn't be staying out late on a regular basis during the week, but I can still drive you on Tuesday and Thursday afternoons, right?'

I smiled. 'Absolutely.'

He had a different CD on this time, which I recognised: Pnau's *Sambanova*. I could not resist turning up the volume and bopping a little. He looked at me briefly and grinned before returning his attention to the road.

'I have this album too,' I explained.

'You are a lady of impeccable taste, my dear.'

Those last two words stood out to me more than anything else he said that trip. I felt it was time to make my own feelings better known with my reply, 'Your own tastes are exquisite, *my dear*.'

He lost his focus briefly then swerved a bit, enraging some other road users around us. He corrected his steering, causing no real harm, so we both chuckled.

We arrived at my house safely and Nick made an exaggerated sigh of relief that sent both of us into a hysterical laughing fit. Once settled, we looked at each other in silent anticipation. I expected him to make his move then, but he looked away, seemingly distracted by the loud bass of a passing car.

I made to exit the car, but Nick grabbed my wrist. 'Will I see you on Thursday?' he asked.

'Yes, of course. Oh, and thank you for the lift to—
'

At that moment, Nick lent across the car and kissed the corner of my mouth.

I shifted my head to bring my lips into full contact with his. He climbed across to my seat to straddle me, then he cupped my face with his hands and enclosed my mouth with his soft lips. The tangy fragrance of his Calvin Klein cologne filled my nostrils, feeding my desire. I gripped his waist and pulled his pelvis closer into my lap. He tasted strongly of spearmint, the likely result of chewing gum. Once my brain had finished analysing my initial senses, I closed my eyes, yielding to his touch so that he could take me away to a dream world.

This lasted for a considerable time, ending only when I heard Mum's Land Rover pulling up into the driveway alongside us.

'Mm... (kiss)... I should... (kiss)... probably... (kiss)... go now... (kiss)... Thank you, Nick.'

'You ... (kiss)... are... (kiss)... *most* welcome... (kiss)... Phoebe.'

࿇

It happened at lunchtime, following fourth period English that Wednesday.

We spent the class on another shared reading of *Like Water for Chocolate*. During this lesson, Mr. Collins called my name, implying that I should continue the story. We were up to chapter three, and it was my task to narrate the aphrodisiac effect of Tita's quail in rose petal sauce recipe upon her sister Gertrudis. I blushed a little when I told the tale of this woman's unbridled desire.

When I paused briefly, I chanced a glance at Mr. Collins and saw his eyes fixed on me intently. Thankfully, everyone else had their head in their book. He prompted me to go on, so I read until the lunch bell sounded.

I always took some care when packing up my books after class, so I was usually the last student out of the room. This day was no exception, and as I walked past the desk of Mr. Collins, he grabbed my arm to hold me back. After locking the door, he pinned me against it with his strong, tall frame. Lifting the skirt of my winter uniform, he whispered those unforgettable words in my ear.

I could not resist Mr. Collins, nor did I want to.

∾∿

Netball practice, my first for the term, was interesting that night. While I saw no evidence of it, I could sense the eyes of Mr. Collins on me much of the time. He also seemed to be working me harder than normal, although this could have been the result of my depleted level of fitness. Toward the end of the session, exhaustion overwhelmed me, and I tripped, hitting the asphalt with my right knee. It stung like hell, and I could see a nasty graze.

Mr. Collins rushed to my aid, dismissing the crowd that was forming around me. 'That's enough gawking ladies. Practice is over now; you can all go home.' He started to help me to straighten my leg out, then the professional part of his brain must have kicked in when he shouted, '*Denise*, you can stay and help with Phoebe's injury.'

She ran back to us, panting. 'Yes Mr. Collins. What should I do?'

'You can start by fetching a first aid kit,' he instructed.

'Yes Mr. Collins. Be right back.' Denise rushed off to the front office.

Mr. Collins filled a nearby bucket with water. When Denise returned with the first aid kit, Mr. Collins soaked a sterile bandage in the water. Kneeling beside me, he used it to rinse the worst of the dirt and gravel from my wound. He used a gauze swab to clean it further and I winced from the pain. Seeing this, he squeezed my hand gently as a sign of support. Finally, he applied a sterile dressing. 'Do you think anything is broken?'

I moved my leg a little. 'No, I don't think so.'

'I want you to try getting up with our help, okay?'
'Okay.'

He gestured for Denise to support my left side, while he took my right arm and placed it over his shoulder. With their help I limped to a nearby bench.

Once I was seated, Mr. Collins addressed Denise again, 'Can you please retrieve an incident report form from the front office?'

'Yes, of course.' She grabbed the first aid kit and returned to reception.

As soon as she was gone, he placed a hand gingerly on my right thigh. 'How are you feeling now?'

I looked directly into his eyes. 'It still hurts a lot but having you here is helping with the pain.'

'I am glad to hear you say that. I was so worried when I saw you fall.' He removed his hand from my leg just in time as Denise returned with the requested paperwork. 'How are you girls planning to get home? It is getting dark.'

'We were planning to catch the bus,' was my reply.

Denise looked at her watch. 'We just missed a bus though and have quite a wait for the next one.'

'Can I offer you both a lift? I would prefer to see that you get home safe.'

I was probably too quick to respond, 'Yes, that would be lovely. Thank you. I don't fancy my chances boarding a bus in this condition anyway.'

We dropped Denise off first, which must have seemed suspicious considering she lived further out of town than me, but she didn't seem to suspect anything.

Mr. Collins then drove to an empty parking lot

near my house. 'How does your leg feel?'

I turned to him, grinning. 'Still a little sore, but much improved.'

He got out of the car, came around to my side and opened the rear door. He then opened my door, lifted me out and laid me down on the back seat. He positioned himself on top of me, taking great care not to hurt my leg. 'Please excuse the location, Phoebe. This is not my usual style, but I fear that we must take advantage of as many opportunities as we get.'

With that, he made me forget the pain of my leg entirely.

Chapter Ten

Diary extract dated Friday 11ᵗʰ May 2001

'Hello Phoebe. I have been meaning to ask, who was that boy from St. Mark's you met after school yesterday?'

Oh God, no! 'That was my friend Nick.'

He started to squeeze my left thigh through my skirt. 'Friend?' he asked with a suspicious tone.

I t is probably worth recounting the phone conversation with Denise following my first kiss with Nick.

'Hi Denise, I have some good news for you!'

'Hi Phoebs. He kissed you, didn't he?'

I laughed. 'Um yeah—how'd you guess?'

'I can hear it in your voice, and I know he just drove you home. But what you haven't told me is *how far*?'

'Denise!' I squealed, 'He is a gentleman and I'm a

lady!'

'How far?' she insisted.

'First base and that's it… *so far.*'

'Hehehe, slow and steady. Nice.'

∞

When Nick drove me home after school on Thursday, I invited him inside. As soon as we reached the front steps he commented, 'The place already looks very nice.'

I thought so too. I always loved this house, a single story, French Provincial style building, with a large white frontage. The ornamental front doors lead into a twenty-foot, square family room that formed the centre of the house.

I gave Nick a tour of the house, stopping in the kitchen on the way though to grab each of us a drink. Leaving my bedroom until last, I made a point of showing off my book collection.

'A very stylish house and your library is most impressive.' Drawing close to me he added, 'This room's my favourite.' Then he enfolded me, and we kissed, returning me to that dreamy place.

We slumped down onto my bed and continued kissing. This time things got a little more heated, but we did not remove any clothing.

The sound of the front door closing brought my awareness back to this world and we sat up. 'That'll be Mum. Ready to meet her?'

'Sure.'

I led Nick back out to the family room. 'Hi Mum, this is Nick. Nick this is my Mum, Laura.'

Mum offered her hand. 'Well, hi Nick. It's good to meet you at last.'

Nick shook Mum's hand. 'Hi Laura. It's a pleasure.'

We all sat down for a drink, and I beamed at the sight of them getting along well.

₭₮

Mr. Collins found me alone in a private study room during on Friday morning. He sat down beside me and questioned me about Nick in a hushed tone. '*Friend*?' he queried.

'Okay, so we have kissed, but that's all. I like him, but....'

'Hmm?'

'I don't know about taking things any further because of you.'

His hand shifted higher up my thigh. 'What we have is a secret, Phoebe. No one can know about us while you are still my student, so I think it would be good for you to have a normal boyfriend *as well*.'

His suggested both relieved and confused me. 'I guess so. You're not upset with me?'

'Upset? No. Just a little disappointed that you did not tell me earlier. I want you to feel that you can talk to me about anything. Let me be the one person you do not have to hide anything from.' He kissed my forehead then stood up with a smile. 'I must get back to my year nine class. I hope I do not return to a riot.'

Chapter Eleven

Diary extract dated Friday 18th May 2001

There was a fire in his eyes that I had never seen before and I wondered if he was angry with me. He looked like a wild animal advancing on its prey. He pushed me back into the cubicle, not violently, but still forcefully. It was obvious that he was overcome with a strong carnal need. He paused only to disrobe, then pounced, seizing his quarry.

O ur long-awaited cinema excursion to see *Chocolat* finally came on Thursday 17th May. The week had not yet given us a chance to meet alone, so I made a point of sitting next to Mr. Collins in the cinema. Because this trip took the place of our final period lesson it also went into the evening.

When the lights dimmed, I felt a familiar hand on my left knee. I looked at him, but his eyes remained focused on the screen. Whatever we did here would have to be subtle because the rest of my English class surrounded us. I could feel his fingers start to scratch at my thigh through my skirt. *How far would he take it in such a public place?* He moved his hand to the very top of my thigh and pried my legs very slightly apart. *Oh god, how was I supposed to focus on this movie?*

I decided that two could play at this game. I moved my hand to his knee and felt a mild jolt in his leg.

He moved his hand further towards its likely destination.

I moved my own hand higher up his leg. I had some catching up to do if I was going to have any chance of winning this race, so I moved faster toward my objective.

He reached the apex of his journey and lingered there waiting for my response.

I squirmed a little, then reached my own finish line.

We both spent the remainder of the movie teasing each other. Unfortunately, this was as far as we could take things that night.

≈≈

I had plans with Nick for a proper date following netball practice the following night. For this reason, I decided to take a shower once the other girls had finished in the change rooms. I wanted the facilities to myself so that I could spread my things out.

Having just turned on the shower, I was about to step under the water, when I heard the outer door of the change room slam shut. Worried that maybe I had been locked in, I stepped out of my cubicle to check. That was when I saw Mr. Collins, in nothing but a bathrobe, storming towards me.

I was a lamb in his clutches, and he rendered me senseless beneath the hot, cascading water.

Once I had sated his voracious appetite, Mr. Collins' fervour subsided, and he kissed me tenderly. 'I am so sorry, Phoebe. I hope that I have not hurt you?'

I felt fine, more than fine actually. My body had been craving this more than I realised. Turning off the shower, I examined myself. 'No serious injuries.'

He looked concerned.

'I'm fine, really.' I returned to his arms. 'More than fine.'

'It is getting late, will you let me drive you home?'

'Nick is picking me up tonight. We have a date.'

He seemed a little uneasy hearing this news but said nothing of it. 'I had best leave you to it then. I will stand guard outside of the changeroom.' Smiling, he added, 'You would not want any strange men barging in now, would you?'

To that I gave him a coy look.

'Watch yourself, young lady. You might not make it out of here in time for your date if you keep taunting me like that.' With that, he left me to my own devices. The problem was, I could not remember how to use them.

ဆဝၑ

My date with Nick comprised dinner at an Italian restaurant, followed by dancing at a club.

The dim, warm ceiling lights, tabletop candles, and soft music gave the dining room a romantic ambience. Nick ordered a bottle of Chardonnay that I found surprisingly pleasant. I had only ever tasted extremely dry white wines since that was how Mum preferred them.

When it came time to select the food, I found it hard to choose. Eating was the last thing on my mind, so I just picked the risotto from the top of the mains.

During the meal, Nick observed, 'You look a bit preoccupied tonight, Phoebe. Is everything okay?'

'I'm fine. Just a little worried about my English… studies.'

He stroked my hand gently. 'Relax my dear. It's Friday night. The weekend is young. You'll have plenty of time to worry about school later.'

I did my best to follow his advice. The wine certainly helped.

The night club, named *The Vault*, was something else. I had been to plenty of underage discos in my time, but this was my first time stepping into a bona fide adult joint. It was a large venue, yet somehow the dancefloor was so densely packed that personal space became a foreign concept. A smoky haze filled the air, intensifying the coloured light beams that were radiating from the stage and ceiling, and scantily clad men and women were dancing next to the DJ and on podiums jutted about the room.

We started by grabbing a drink from the bar. 'I'm gonna avoid alcohol and stick to energy drinks tonight,' I told him. 'I want to enhance the feeling of excitement this place gives me, not dampen it.'

He grinned. 'Good plan.'

Next, we toured the place, discovering that there were about five separate rooms, each with a different style of electronic music playing.

Nick and I agreed to start in the main area where the DJ was playing some familiar sounding Euro-trance. I danced harder than ever before, bouncing around and frequently bumping into my neighbours, none of whom seemed to care. Nick was really in his element here, often closing his eyes to lose himself in the music.

I stayed over at Nick's that night, and while I did not technically need Mum's consent, she was still completely fine with the idea. Our relationship was one built on trust, and she believed I would not do anything stupid. She also really liked Nick. I had already met Nick's parents, Frank and Selina, both relaxed people who respected our privacy— something that was easy to do in a house that size. It was a beautiful old Tudor style building verging on mansion. It even had wings!

When we got to Nick's room, he pulled me down on his bed, kissing me for a while. Then he stood abruptly. 'I'm going to put my PJs on. Do you have any to change into?'

This came as a surprise. I had not anticipated the need for bed clothes this evening. Blushing, I replied, 'Um, no, I forgot.'

He reached into his clothing drawers and produced an old tracksuit set. 'Here, you can borrow these.'

He then walked out of the room to change, leaving me dumbfounded. *Was he for real?* This eighteen-year-old guy was acting primmer and more proper than my forty-year-old English teacher. He even knocked before entering to ensure that I had finished dressing. I wondered if he was a virgin.

After a spell of canoodling in his bed I could feel his yearning, so I attempted to remove his trousers. He brought his hand down to stop me. 'I really want you Phoebe, more than you would believe. But I also have other strong feelings for you, so, I think we should take things slowly.'

'Hmm, I think I understand.' Although not all of me agreed with his sentiment. 'So, what are our limits tonight?'

'Let's treat tonight as a "dress rehearsal." So long as the clothes stay on, anything goes.'

Chapter Twelve

'You know the rules, Phoebe, so I do not think it is necessary to instruct you on them. Now what do you have to say for yourself?' He seemed really pissed.

'I'm sorry Mr. Collins. It won't happen again.'

'I also detest the idea of routine disciplinary action for you. No, I have something else in mind.'

I was not accustomed to reprimand in class; in fact, I was somewhat proud of my scrupulous record thus far. It was also unusual for me to forget basic protocol, such as turning off my mobile phone and putting it away at school, but something was changing in me, and I was sure it related to my sexual awakening. My afternoon English lesson was, therefore, quite out of the ordinary.

Quiet reading time occupied our time, working

our way through *Like Water for Chocolate*, when the familiar sound of a mobile phone message tone sounded from within my blazer pocket: *Bah-dah-be be-be be-be-beep. Bah-dah-be be-be be-be-beep.*

Mr. Collins, who had been pacing through the room and just passing my desk at the time, spun around, and glared at me. All other eyes in the room fixed on me too. I could not imagine what colour my faced turned thereupon because I felt flush with embarrassment and frozen in terror.

Putting his hand out towards me, palm facing up, Mr. Collins demanded, 'I will take that for now, thank you Phoebe.'

A few sniggers erupted around me. Wishing I could just shrink away into my chair, I handed him my phone.

'You can collect it from me after school.' He switched my phone off and placed it in his pocket.

The rest of the class returned to their reading, but I remained frozen. *How could I be so stupid?* Knowing that I had angered Mr. Collins distressed me and I feared the impact this would have on our relationship.

The final bell sounded, releasing me from my musings, and the rest of the girls rushed out of class. I remained in my seat.

Mr. Collins locked the door, then sat on the edge of my desk. He removed my phone from his pocket, turned it back on and read the offending text message aloud, 'Let me see here. Ah, here it is. "HI MY DEAR. CAN'T MEET U 2NIGHT SOZ BUT WILL PICK U UP @5 ON SAT FOR DINS & MOVIE @ WESTSIDE PLAZA XX NICK." Intriguing.' He handed it back to me and chided me in a firm tone.

I grinned. 'What type of punishment do you have in mind, Mr. Collins?'

'I would like you to remove your panties, then kneel on the floor, facing away from me.'

I obeyed his instructions.

I heard the tell-tale sound of a belt buckle unfasten, followed by fabric dropping to the floor, then he knelt close behind me. His warm hand settled on my backside, rubbing it vigorously. 'I would like to spank you, Phoebe. Would you object?'

I gulped. *Oh wow, this was next level.* 'No Mr. Collins, I would not object.'

Smack. His hand resumed the rubbing. 'How did that feel?'

'It stung a bit, but... it felt good... arousing.'

'Mm, I had hoped as much. May I spank you again?'

'Yes.'

'Please tell me to stop if this becomes too much for you, okay Phoebe?'

'Okay.' I was beginning to feel moist between my legs.

He struck me another five times before taking me. This was a punishment I could get used to.

'I would like more opportunities to punish you like that, Phoebe. I permit you to infringe upon a few minor rules in my class on future occasions.'

'You want me to break the rules *openly*?'

'Sporadically, yes. And only insignificant offences such as passing notes, talking in class, chewing gum, or breaking the uniform policy.'

I agreed, wondering just how far he wanted to venture down this new avenue of our relationship and what I would accept.

Chapter Thirteen

Diary extract dated Saturday 26th May 2001

The "Awkward Threesome" started over dinner...

'Hello Phoebe. You look lovely tonight. Who is this dashing young man on your arm?'

Nick and I had just walked up to the entrance of the café where I found none other than Mr. Collins sitting at a table out the front. *Oh no, what was he thinking, and how did he know?* Casting my mind back, I swiftly remembered the incident in class.

'Hi Mr. Collins. This is Nick.' I began searching for some reason to explain the obvious familiarity.

Mr. Collins extended a hand towards Nick. 'Hi Nick. Please, call me Jonah.'

Nick looked a little puzzled as he shook hands with Mr. Collins.

'Mr. Collins, or rather Jonah here, is a good family friend.'

Mr. Collins gave me a sly look at that.

'Ah, hello Jonah. A pleasure to meet you. May we join you?' Nick was always friendly to a fault and tonight was a classic example, but he had no idea what he was facilitating here.

Grinning, Mr. Collins replied, 'Certainly, I would be most obliged.'

So, we sat down to dine, and I looked on as a witness to my two worlds colliding.

'You know what, Nick? Phoebe here has not told you everything about us yet.'

What the? I almost lost my mouthful of food then. *Why was he doing this?*

'You see, I am also her English teacher at school. I know she would be too modest to admit this, but she is an exceptional student.'

Nick placed his arm around my waist and smiled at me warmly. 'I can believe that Jonah. She's an exceptional girl.'

The conversation shifted into safer topics for the remainder of the meal and my anxiety eased. Just as we were finishing our drinks, Mr. Collins asked, 'So, what did the two of you have planned next? I am going to see a movie myself.'

Seriously? Was he planning to chaperone our entire date?

'Ah, so are we. I'm taking Phoebe to see *Moulin Rouge.*'

'What a coincidence. I was planning to see that very same film. I am quite a fan of Baz Luhrmann.'

It seemed this *was* his intention.

'Well Jonah, you should join us. Movies aren't as much fun to watch alone.'

'A most accurate sentiment, Nick. You are very kind, thank you.'

When Nick was busy in the candy bar, I stepped close to Mr. Collins and whispered, 'What are you playing at Jonah?'

'I see no harm in a little sport, *my dear*. Nick is a charming lad by the way—so... accommodating.'

Nick led us into the cinema, choosing a seat up the back. Mr. Collins sat next to me, positioning me in between the two of them. Nick made a point of lifting the armrest blocking access to me, then snuggled in close.

Once the lights dimmed, Mr. Collins surreptitiously moved the armrest on his side. My predicament was thus: Nick's arms embracing me on the right, and Mr. Collins' hand on my left thigh. I resigned to play this tantalising game, *come what may*, so I put my hands on each of their legs.

When the end credits started to roll, Mr. Collins and I promptly withdrew our hands from each other's person, and Nick appeared none the wiser for it. It was time for this *crowd* to disperse, so Nick and I bid Mr. Collins farewell and headed back to Nick's home.

The intimacy increased that night, likely due to the sensual quality of the evening's entertainment, the ancillary action, or presumably both. The moment that Nick closed his bedroom door he seized me. Our kissing was intense and fitful while he disarrayed me.

Once naked, I lay back on his bed. Pausing, he took in the view for a moment, then walked over to his stereo to put some trance music on. He began to undress, then noticing how attentive I was, he lessened the pace to make a show if it. His shirt came off, exposing a hairless, muscular chest with a good tan. The sight captivated me and my body temperature rose. The pants gave way to reveal designer boxers that did little to conceal the extent of his manhood. This was where the spectacle ended, however, because Nick was upon me in a flash.

His hands were the first to fully explore my body and I writhed excitably in response to his touch. Then he took his mouth for the tour, which ended in full lip service.

Chapter Fourteen

Diary extract dated Saturday 16th June 2001

I closed my eyes and pressed my lips against his, but I was still trembling, so I accidently bit him. His tongue traced the site of the wound then he thrust it into my mouth, introducing the bitter, metallic taste of his blood, mixed with the salty tang of my tears. I could feel his hands gripping my shoulder blades, his fingers digging in. My own hands pressed against his chest, and I could feel his heart beating incredibly strong and fast. This kiss felt more real than any that came before.

It may seem like I have been skipping ahead in my narrative at times. While it is true that I have not been giving a full account of my daily interactions with the significant people in my life, I feel that not all of these are pertinent to my retelling. This is not to say that such moments were unimportant.

My clandestine encounters in the classroom with

Mr. Collins became frequent, usually preceded by the excuse given to my friends that I needed quiet study time.

I continued to accept a lift home with Nick after school most Tuesdays and Thursdays and we enjoyed numerous dates on weekends, some of which were double dates with Denise and Curtis.

Denise had progressed well with Curtis and they were sleeping together several nights a week by this stage. Whenever I spent the night with Nick, Denise would ring me the next day for the details. Calling me following my *Moulin Rouge* date, she started with, 'Hi Phoebs. Have you guys done it yet?'

I laughed. 'Not yet. We did reach third base though.'

'My God, he is slow! Okay, now tell me the deets.'

ඩඥ

Curtis had become a regular spectator at our Saturday morning netball games, a favour that Denise frequently returned by going to his squash matches. Nick was finally able to join him on June 16th and I was thrilled to have him there.

After greeting me with a hug, Nick looked past me and asked, 'Hey, is that Jonah?'

I turned to see Mr. Collins a short distance away, waving. 'Yes, he's my coach.'

He paused to process this. 'Let me get this straight—Jonah's a family friend, your teacher, and your netball coach?'

'Yes, that's right.'

'No wonder you guys are so close.'

He didn't know the half of it!

With the game was about to start, I made my way on court, but not without noticing Nick talking to Mr. Collins. I was curious to know what they were discussing but decided not to get distracted from my game. The team had been performing well this season and I was on Wing Attack that day, so I was not about to let them down.

At half time we were slightly ahead on thirty-seven goals. I felt pretty good about our game. We were all playing well, and I hadn't yet missed a single pass. After a brief pep talk with the team, Mr. Collins pulled me aside. 'You have remarkable form today, Phoebe.'

I knew his complement was an intentional double entendre, so I smiled at him demurely.

The second half of the game went even better for us, our opponents clearly tiring. We brought victory home with a twenty-goal lead. I hugged my teammates, then ran to Nick and embraced him.

'Congratulations my dear. You played really well.' Then he kissed me there in the open.

This was our first public display and it was right in front of Mr. Collins. It didn't occur to me until afterwards just how hard it must have been for Mr. Collins to witness. But the pained expression he gave me just after the kiss hinted at the effect it had on him.

Nick and Curtis took us out for a celebratory drink, which would have felt a lot more festive if I didn't keep thinking of that look Mr. Collins gave me. I needed to know that things were still okay between us. After a couple of rounds, I explained that I really needed to study. Nick offered me a lift home, but I told him I wanted to use the public library in the city to do some research. Once I was a safe distance away, I rang Mr. Collins.

'Hello Phoebe.'

Trembling I replied, 'Hi… Jonah. Can I see you?'

'Is everything okay Phoebe? Where are you?' He sounded worried.

'I… I hope so. I'm near the netball courts.'

'Really? I thought you left with your *boyfriend*.'

The way he said that last word stung, and I knew that he was not happy.

'I did, but…'

'Wait there. I will come and get you.'

He didn't take long, so I guessed he only just left the place. I jumped straight into his car and he started driving. 'What is wrong Phoebe?'

By this stage I was on the verge of tears and I barely knew why. 'I… I don't know. The way you looked at me after I kissed Nick… I got worried that… I'm sorry Jonah.'

Then the flood gates opened. He stopped the car

on the roadside, lent across the front seat, and placed his arm behind my neck. 'Oh Phoebe, I am sorry. I did not realise… Seeing how happy you were…'

I looked across at him expectantly, still sobbing.

He continued, 'I feared… losing you.'

That was it. I unbuckled my seatbelt and climbed into his lap. My forehead rested on his, my tears trickling down his face. 'I… I'm still here Jonah.'

That was when I closed my eyes to kiss him.

I opened my eyes as I drew my head back for a breath. His own gaze locked with mine, the pupils of his dark brown eyes dilating, and we searched each other's souls. I sensed ardour, devotion, and salacity in his. Mine felt fervour, admiration, and yearning for him. I rested my head against his chest and closed my eyes again, taking in the spicy scent of his cologne. He wrapped his arms around me, and we remained this way for about an hour.

It was Mr. Collins who broke the silence, 'May I take you back to my place, Phoebe?'

'Yes please.'

I spent that whole night at the home of Mr. Collins, then I awoke feeling refreshed and positive. Whilst discussing our favourite topic at the breakfast bar, he asked, 'What books have you chosen to focus on for your independent study?'

'*Dangerous Liaisons*—the English version, of course. Also, the translation of Sade's *The Crimes of Love*. I haven't decided on a third.'

Raising an eyebrow, he remarked, 'I see that your taste for the classics has become more libertine of late.'

I gave him a suggestive look. 'Hmm, I wonder why that might be.'

'Oh Phoebe, you do incite me so.' With that he picked me up and carted me back to bed.

ॐ

Mum appeared distressed when I arrived home later that afternoon, ambushing me the moment I walked in the door.

'Where were you last night, Phoebe? And before you try to pull the wool over my eyes, you should know that Nick and Denise called the house looking for you, so I know you weren't with either of them.'

I sank into the couch and looked at her blankly for a moment. *What on earth could I tell her? Sorry Mum, I was sleeping with my English teacher?* Then I remembered that Dad was usually happy to cover for me. 'I went to Dad's because I needed his help with my English studies.'

Mum let out a sigh of relief. 'Oh, thank God. Why didn't you just call me? I was worried sick.'

'Sorry Mum, it was kinda spur of the moment and I got absorbed in my work.'

'I'm gonna go ring that man and have a word about keeping me in the loop.'

She walked off towards the phone, so I quickly

grabbed my mobile and sent Dad a warning text, SORRY DAD. PLEASE COVER FOR ME.

Once their phone call ended, I got his reply, NO PROBS. YOU OWE ME AN EXPLANATION SOMETIME THOUGH.

Chapter Fifteen

Diary extract dated Thursday 21st June 2001

I'm aghast and completely dumbfounded! I got a "B" for my English paper? This is the first time I got anything short of an "A" in English.

E ven Mr. Collins looked disappointed when he handed back my report on *Like Water for Chocolate.* There was a sticky note attached to it containing feedback that was obviously not meant to go on the official records. It read:

Your analytical and writing standards are slipping, my dear. I sensed that you rushed this one. Too many distractions, perhaps? Please see me about this later.

I did just that. I stayed to see him after class that day. He didn't bother closing the door for this conversation, so I guessed he wasn't in the mood for anything more than talking. He was sitting in his chair, and I sat on the edge of his desk, more out of habit than as a conscious act. The hem of my skirt shifted up markedly as I perched myself there, diverting his eyes as we spoke.

'I will confess that I was quite disappointed by your report, Phoebe.'

'I am sorry Mr. Collins. I kind of left this one to the last minute.' Since his desk wasn't visible from the hallway, I decided to have a little fun with this distraction. I started to gradually lift my skirt higher up my thigh.

'I expect…' he gulped as the skirt moved further up, 'better… next time.'

My panties were visible by this stage. He moved his eyes back up and fixed them on mine. I could see that he was still displeased with me, but that familiar hunger was there too. He quickly pulled my hem down to my knees and whispered, 'Enough. You will have me ruined at this rate.'

I smiled broadly as I said in a hushed tone, 'Tomorrow night then?'

I left it at that and walked out the room. I was beginning to have a lot of fun playing the impish flirt with Mr. Collins, especially knowing the affect it had on his libido.

ℰ൦ℰ

After ravishing me furiously that Friday night, Mr.

Collins expressed genuine concern for my lower grade on the assignment. I curled up in his arms as he spoke. 'Seriously though Phoebe, I do worry that you have been too distracted to focus on your studies lately.'

I sighed. 'I suppose you're right.' I didn't like where this was going.

'If you want my advice, I recommend cutting back on school night outings.'

I knew he was referring to my dates with Nick. 'The problem is, Jonah, if I see Nick less during the week, then I will need to see him more on weekends. That means less time with you.'

'I am not going to dictate how you spend your spare time, Phoebe, but as far as schoolwork goes, this is crunch-time and I do not want to see you throw away your potential.'

He was right, of course. I just didn't want to admit it or face the fact that I would have to see less of Nick and Mr. Collins. They both meant a lot to me in their own different ways. Nick was easy going and gentle with me, but I needed the contrast that Mr. Collins offered me too. I was just going to have to learn how to juggle. After kissing him gently on the cheek, I offered a reassuring smile. 'I promise to return more focus to my studies, Jonah.'

He seemed satisfied with that and reverted his attentions to my body.

Chapter Sixteen

Diary extract dated Friday 29th June 2001

Yr 12 Retreat was amazing! So much fun (despite the drama).

WHen the school announced the Year Twelve Retreat plans, I could barely contain my excitement. Our previous years' retreats had only been one day without any overnight stays, and we had not been on camp since Year Eight. We were going away for three nights this time and the boys at St. Mark's would join us. And, of course, our Homegroup teachers would attend. Mr. Collins even chanced a wink at me when he handed me the notice.

The bus ride out of town took about one hour and we spent much of this time gossiping. Denise and I were not the only girls in our year to have boyfriends at St. Mark's and the girls in our circle who did not were still keen to hear everything about the guys we dated and their friends. Mr. Collins made a point of sitting across the aisle from me and Denise, exposing himself to some awkward truths.

Justine prompted the conversation. 'Denise and Phoebe are dating two of the best-looking guys from that school. Perhaps I will get a chance to hook up with one of their friends?'

I noticed that Mr. Collins' ears pricked up at the mention of me and Nick.

Denise was quick to reply, 'Oh my God babe— yes, I can totally set you up. There is Chad, Drew, Tyler, Justin, and Shane. I think they are all currently single, but Shane just came out of a relationship, so I wouldn't go there unless you wanna be a rebound gal.'

Our friend, Samantha, giggled then and jumped into the conversation. 'Tyler isn't single anymore, hun. We got together on the weekend. I just hadn't had a chance to tell anyone yet.'

Denise beamed. 'Oh wow, that is awesome Sam! Congrats.'

I remembered meeting Tyler at Curtis' birthday. He seemed nice enough, so I chimed in on the congratulations.

Samantha then went on to add, 'Tyler is amazing in the sack and an incredible kisser to boot. So, how well do Curtis and Nick perform?'

Denise replied first of course, 'Curtis is the bomb! He gets me off every time and he is huge.'

'Oh, how big?' Samantha inquired.

Denise used her hands for a size guide. 'Like 10 inches.'

A few of the other girls stared at Denise in amazement. I also noticed Mr. Collins stiffen in his seat. This topic was clearly making him uncomfortable.

'Doesn't that ever hurt?' Justine asked.

Denise grinned at the attention she was getting as she answered, 'Nope.'

Lucy, who I knew to be dating Ben, another student from St. Marks, piped up at this point. 'So, Phoebe, what's it like with Nick? He looks so dreamy.'

I blushed at this. 'Ben is pretty cute too, aren't you happy with him?'

'Of course, but your guy is a top tier babe. He looks like a model, so I'm just curious to know if his looks translate well in the bedroom.'

I had never thought about it objectively that way. I had always found Nick attractive, but it had never occurred to me that I would be making other girls jealous. All eyes were on me, so I told them, 'Nick is a great boyfriend, and he wants to take things slow.' I tried to keep my own stories of Nick to a minimum out of respect for Mr. Collins.

'Wait, you haven't done it yet?' came Samantha's shocked reply.

'No, we haven't yet.' And I left it at that.

When our bus arrived at the site of the retreat, a

lovely Spanish style villa, the boys of St. Mark's College formally greeted us in four neat lines. It took all my self-control to remain calm and not rush into Nick's arms when I spotted him, and I could see Denise fidgeting at the sight of Curtis. We both knew that this was not the time or place to make a scene.

With the first of these formalities out of the way, a teacher guided us to our rooms so that we could deposit our luggage and settle in before the first session. Two dormitories flanked the main function area of the campsite. We knew our accommodation was going segregate us from the boys, but a pang of disappointment clenched at my heart when I saw the massive distance between our lodgings. Denise and I found a bunk to share that was near the bathroom, then proceeded to unpack.

It amazed me how much Denise managed to fit into her smart brown Louis Vuitton case and matching duffle bag. There was a range of dresses (more than we needed for the trip), each with matching shoes, an entire makeup kit, a selection of perfumes, a designer negligee and coordinating silk robe, a discman with a few CDs, snacks, and a full toiletries kit.

My own luggage, a neat black & white damask bag, only had a couple of tracksuits, a little black dress with coordinating designer jacket and dress shoes, comfy PJs, dressing gown and slippers, two paperback books, a hair straightener, my Gucci perfume, headache pills, a bit of makeup, and a few toiletries.

∞∞

Once we had all gathered in the conference room, we received our program booklets, which contained the full agenda and workbook space for each session. It was then time for Name Bingo, our icebreaker activity. For this game, we each needed to find different names that matched sixteen different criteria like "Someone who is left-handed," "Someone who likes reading comics," "Someone who loves to dance," and "Someone who plays tennis." When our grids were complete, we would use them to play an actual game of bingo. Most of us groaned when the rules were first explained to us, but it turned out to be a lot of fun.

Straight up, I knew plenty of people who liked to dance and two guys who played tennis. The other criteria were harder to fill out, so I asked around. 'Hi Tyler, good to see you again.'

'Yeah likewise, Phoebe.'

'So, do any of these apply to you?' I asked, pointing to the squares that I had not yet ticked.

He looked them over for a bit. 'I'm actually pretty good at Math. I don't know what month you were born in, but I'm an October baby.'

I smiled warmly, 'That makes two of us. What date in October?'

'The eleventh. How 'bout you?' he inquired.

'Oh my God—I'm the twelfth! We are like a day apart!' He raised his hand for a high-five. 'Go team October!'

'So, we can both tick that square off our grids. Who else do you know that's good at Math in your school?'

He looked around conspiratorially, then replied, 'Drew is an actual genius in math and science, but he would kick my ass if he knew I told you.'

I laughed at that. I never did understand guys wanting to dumb themselves down to look cool. Being smart had no impact on popularity in my own school. 'Thanks Tyler, Drew's secret is safe with me. By the way, I heard about you hooking up with Samantha. Congrats on that.'

He grinned, then caught Sam's eye and they blew each other kisses. 'Thanks Phoebe, see ya round?'

'Of course. Bye Tyler.'

∩⊃

After lunch, we formed teams to work with for the retreat. I ended up with Denise, Justine, Samantha, Lucy, Nick, Curtis, Drew, Tyler, and Ben.

The team-building games followed, the first of which was Pictionary. This was where I learnt that Nick was also good at drawing and Curtis clearly wasn't! Nick sat close to me throughout this game, such that our legs were touching, and he would often hold my hand, releasing it only when a teacher passed by, or when he needed to draw. This contact was driving me so crazy that when it was my turn to draw, I couldn't get my mind off sex, especially when the word I needed to draw was "Inside." I blushed and giggled as I took my word card.

Mr. Collins arched a brow at my reaction, walked up to me and grabbed the card to check what it was. I could see him stifle a smile—an expression that I doubted anyone else caught. 'Honestly, Phoebe, get your mind out of the gutter.' A few snickers sounded about the room. 'And the same goes for the rest of you.' Passing the card back, he brushed my hand with his own, sending sparks through my body and plunging my mind even further south. He prompted me to continue with my turn.

For the second game, we formed a circle with our team. Then we had to join hands with people across the circle and work together to untangle ourselves without letting go. I ended up with one hand joined to Lucy's and the other in Ben's enormous grip. He was holding my hand firmly and occasionally squeezed it to get my attention. Each time he did this, I would find him smiling at me, setting off the first of my internal alarm bells. Unwelcome gestures aside, the game was a lot of fun, and we were able to work so well as a team that we won.

ॐ

Mr. Collins caught me alone when I was on my way to the bathroom during break time. He quickly grabbed my hand and pulled me into a private alcove. After kissing me deeply, he spoke softly, 'Watching you and listening to you today has been driving me wild, Phoebe. Meet me in the garden tonight after lights-out.'

My heart was racing when I whispered, 'With pleasure, Mr. Collins.'

He gave me one of those sly grins, reserved only for me, then released me from his clutches.

When I was sure that everyone else was asleep that night, I slipped quietly out of bed, pausing briefly to don my dressing gown and slippers, then stole out of the dormitory, failing to notice Lucy's empty bed on my way. The moon offered little light that night, so I was able to keep to the shadows, moving slowly so as not to trip on the unfamiliar terrain.

A young male voice caught me unawares as I crept into an artificially lit part of the garden. 'Well if it isn't Phoebe. I was hoping to catch you alone this week.'

I jumped. *Oh shit!* It was Ben. He was sitting on the concrete bench next to the fountain.

'Um, hi Ben. What are you doing here?'

'I'm just waiting for Lucy; I think she's lost. What are *you* doing here, Phoebe? I happen to know Nick is tucked away sound asleep now. So, who are you sneaking out to meet, hmm?'

I hesitated a moment before replying, 'No one, just taking a walk because I couldn't sleep.'

'You don't fool me, Phoebe. I can tell you are up to no good. Come on, who is it?'

I remained silent, unsure how to get out of this mess.

He took my silence for guilt, then continued, 'It's okay Phoebe, I know your secret.'

Oh God! My heart started thumping, and my palms were sweating despite the cold night air. 'You do?' I asked nervously.

'Of course. You must've seen Lucy leaving, so you figured I'd be out here. You came looking for me. But that's ok, because I want you too, babe.'

I was both relieved and horrified at his false assumption. Before I could stop him, Ben grabbed me, pulled me down into his lap, his arms firmly around me as his lips pressed upon my own, and his vulgar tongue found its way into my mouth. I tried to push him away, but he was far too strong for me.

Finally, the sound of a twig snapping released me from this torture. We both looked up to find Mr. Collins standing over us. I was so thankful for his arrival, but then I noticed his look of dismay. *Oh no!* He must have thought that I wanted this kiss. '*What* do the two of you think you are doing out of bed at this time of night! Ben, is it?'

He anxiously nodded as he replied, 'Yes sir, sorry

sir.'

'I will be having words with your Headmaster first thing tomorrow, but for now, get back to your bed this instant.'

He was up in a flash, leaving me to fend for myself as I tumbled out of his lap, scrambling to maintain my balance.

Mr. Collins sat down next to me, gripping my hand. '*What* the blazing hell was that Phoebe?'

'An unwanted assault, I promise you. He caught me out here and assumed I was looking for him since Nick was in bed. He was too strong for me to pull away. I hate to imagine what else he would have tried if you hadn't shown up when you did.'

His expression changed from anger to remorse. 'Oh, Phoebe, I am so sorry. Come, let us find a more... private spot to talk.' He embraced me as he said this, then helped me to my feet.

'Wait, what about Lucy? Ben mentioned that she was going to meet him here.'

'Do not worry. I caught her snooping around and sent her back to bed.'

With that settled, I followed him into the depths of the garden.

&)(&

Remaining true to his word, Mr. Collins spoke to Ben's Headmaster and the suspension that followed, effective immediately, was of much comfort to me because I did not fancy seeing him again that week. Strangely, Lucy was not overly upset by the news of her boyfriend's expulsion from camp. Mr. Collins also assured me that he kept my name out of the report, stating that he caught Ben alone after he had already sent Lucy back to bed. He did not, however, follow up on any further disciplinary action for Lucy until after the retreat.

The small group discussion after breakfast on Wednesday was of much interest. Each group discussed examples of social injustice that we had been witnessed in our own lives. We needed to choose one of these to present to the larger group by describing how the principles of social justice could be applied to improve the situation.

Nick got the ball rolling for us on this one. 'The mistreatment of homeless guys in the city is a classic example. Most people just ignore them, but I have seen other people ridicule them and even get violent with them.'

Lucy broke in then. 'There's nothing wrong with shunning those losers, though—right? There's no way I'd be giving them my cash when they are just gonna go and spend it on alcohol anyway.'

I couldn't believe what I was hearing. 'I think that is Nick's point, Lucy. Even that attitude is a social injustice. They are still human beings who deserve the same rights as us. There are lots of different reasons why people end up on the streets and you don't know their personal story or what it's like in their shoes, so you are in no place to judge them for their situation.'

Nick smiled at me. 'So eloquently put my dear.'

This stunned Lucy into silence.

Denise broke the tension. 'I have another example. I recently learnt that my cousin is gay, and his school gave him a hard time when he came out.'

Curtis responded, 'That is a good example. In theory, I don't have a problem with gays, but I don't know how I would react if one of my mates came out at school.'

There was a sound of mutual agreement in the group. After thinking on this a moment, I put in my bit, 'I think the important thing to remember is that we all try to learn tolerance of people who are different to ourselves. If we can extend this to compassion, then that is better still.'

The discussion continued for a while, then the group settled on the example of sexuality for our group presentation, nominating Nick and myself as speakers.

∞∞

We spent free time on Wednesday night playing a game that Curtis instigated. It was a passing game that required all participants to sit in a circle. Once we were in place, he explained, 'The aim is to pass a lollipop around the circle, using only our mouths.'

This got a lot of laughs and howls from the group.

First it went from Curtis to Denise and remained locked between their lips for a few minutes, before Denise passed it on to me. Several guys cheered wildly when our lips met, introducing the tangy flavour of the candy into my mouth. The transfer was a little awkward, but we managed it.

Nick was next and this was much easier. He moved in and embraced me for the exchange, sending sparks through my body. We also paused a bit, before I released it into Nick's mouth.

Lucy was next in line and looked a little too eager for my liking. She was leaning in and smiling, with her breasts practically falling out of her low-cut top. Nick tried to release it quickly, but she wasn't pulling away when he did, and the lollipop fell into her cleavage. A few of the guys roared and insisted that she leave it there for the next person, so she did exactly that. After giving Nick a pout, she turned to Justine and the game continued.

Denise caught me alone for a moment afterwards. 'That was a lotta fun huh?'

'Yes,' I replied with a laugh.

'Although Lucy was way outta line, making the moves on Nick like that.'

So, it wasn't just me who noticed. I tried to shrug it off. 'Meh, I'm not worried. Nick doesn't seem the slightest bit into her, and I trust him completely.'

Denise smiled. 'I'm glad, but that still wasn't cool.'

೫೦೧೩

During our free time following supper on the Thursday night a group of us were sitting around chatting when Lucy dropped a bombshell. 'So, Nick, did you know that your girl was cheating on you with my guy the other night?'

I was drinking a hot chocolate at the time and sprayed the contents of my mouth across the room. 'What the fuck, Lucy?' I demanded.

Nick went pale as he asked, 'What are you talking about Lucy?'

'Ben rang me earlier today and confessed to me. He was very apologetic. He told me that Mr. Collins busted them both snogging in the garden, which is why he was suspended.'

Nick turned to me aghast.

I begged him to listen to reason. 'It's not true, Nick. I swear. If it were, why wasn't I suspended?'

Lucy jumped at the opportunity to further defame me. 'I'm guessing its because you are Mr. Collins' pet.'

Nick grabbed my arm and excused us from the group, pulling me aside. 'Why would Lucy make something like that up?'

'Ben forced himself on me when he found me taking a walk in the garden. Thankfully, Mr. Collins saved me from any further violations.'

His expression changed, but he remained pale. 'Shoot! I'm sorry for doubting you Phoebe. But why didn't you tell me?'

'I knew he was your friend, and I didn't want to cause trouble. I begged Mr. Collins not to take the matter any further.'

Nick kissed me lightly on the forehead, then held me in his arms for a while. When we returned to the group, Nick cleared the matter up for me. Lucy did not appear pleased by this news, but it shut her up.

Chapter Seventeen

Diary extract dated Tuesday 3rd July 2001

'Hello Phoebe. Thank you for seeing me.' Mrs. Foster, the school counsellor smiled warmly as she greeted me. It did little to alleviate my anxiety. Why had she summoned me?

'Please take a seat.'

I sat down on the comfortable, grey couch that was clearly designed to make students feel at home.

'A concerned friend approached me this morning. She worries that you are being mistreated by one of your teachers.'

During the school term I complied with Mr. Collins's request to break a few minor rules. Every occasion provoked him to unleash his darker passions, each time more intense than the previous. The first of these, following the phone incident, was when I chose to keep chewing my gum in class instead of putting it in the bin as normal. This earnt me eight firm strikes on the backside with some very heated follow up.

This game gave me a huge adrenaline rush, much like the scariest show rides, but this time the thrill mixed with another kind of surge as well. I could feel myself becoming easily addicted, so I made a point of restricting the playtime.

The next time was on a Friday afternoon during a Pastoral Care session. This gave me an opportunity to pass a note to Denise. She knew I'd had a date with Nick the previous night and had been trying to get the details from me all day. I gave them to her in note form.

Okay, okay, here are the deets from last night:

*Nick kissed me wildly, then tore my clothes off.

*He went downstairs.

*Then I went downstairs.

*That was as far as we got.

I made sure to pass the note to her just as Mr. Collins looked at me. It got the desired effect, earning me 10 strikes. He also thanked me for keeping him abreast of things with Nick.

The game was getting intoxicatingly fun, so I decided to be more brazen during the last week of school for that term. On Monday night I snuck into Mum's sewing room and hemmed my skirt just above regulation length. I was hoping for a two-fold effect on Mr. Collins and it did not go unnoticed. At the end of home room that Tuesday morning he stopped me. 'Phoebe, I need to speak to you about your breach of the uniform policy. Please stay back here for your free period this morning.'

Denise and I looked at each other and she smiled apologetically. She had noticed my adjustment on the bus that morning and praised my courage.

When the room had emptied of everyone but Mr. Collins and me, he locked the door, and turned on his jazz CD. Playing music was something he often did when working alone in his classroom, and it was great for masking any noises we made. As he approached my desk, the look in his eyes was one of pure lasciviousness and I knew I was in for some special treatment.

'You are becoming more wanton by the day, Miss Braddock. Please bare yourself for the punishment.' This time he struck me with more force than before. He had reached fifteen and was still going when we heard a knock at the door.

We both froze, then Justine's voice called out, 'Mr.

Collins? Are you there? It's Justine.'

We knew there was no point hiding his presence because of the music. I quickly composed myself, returned to my seat, and pretended to study before he opened the door.

Justine glanced at me before looking back at him. 'Why was the door locked, Mr. Collins?'

'I do not know Justine; it must have jammed somehow. Now what can I help you with?' He did an exceptional job of hiding any anxiety in his voice.

'I left my blazer on my chair and just wanted to grab it.'

I was finding it hard to hide the pain I felt with my stinging cheeks against the chair.

When Justine passed me, she whispered, 'Are you okay Phoebs?'

I mumbled, 'Aha.'

Seemingly satisfied by my reply, she left with her blazer.

Once gone, Mr. Collins shut the door and we both exhaled. I jumped out of my seat to ease the pressure. I had not yet put my panties back on and felt that doing so at this point would just add to the pain, so I slipped them from my tightly clutched hand into my pocket.

Mr. Collins was standing against the door, still trying to settle his breathing.

I pressed myself up close against him to whisper, 'That was too close.' I winced as I added, 'Also, this sadistic little game is going to have to stop. My backside is still stinging.'

He put his arms around me. 'Oh, my dear Phoebe. I am so sorry.' His voice betrayed deep anguish and remorse. 'I promise I will never hit you again.' He lifted my chin and kissed me softly.

ℰᏝℭᏝ

The school counsellor summoned me to her office at lunch time that day. I stared at her blankly, refusing to divulge any emotions.

Mrs. Foster continued, 'Your safety is of the utmost importance to me and the school leadership team. If someone is taking advantage of you, we can protect you, I promise.'

I silently considered my options.

She went on, 'If you have been subjected to any unsolicited physical contact, please do not feel afraid to tell me.'

Well at least this wouldn't be lying. 'It's okay Mrs. Foster. No one has mishandled me. This concerned friend must have been mistaken.'

'Are you sure dear?'

I smiled, hoping to convince her. 'Yes, quite sure.'

'Well, if you are certain, then I will let you go, but please don't hesitate to see me if you feel the need to talk about *anything*.'

My heart was racing when I left that room. I had to fight against the strong urge to rush to Mr. Collins with the story because I knew it would make the situation worse. I decided to wait until I could ring him that night.

He sounded worried when he answered the phone. 'Is everything okay Phoebe?'

This only added to my own apprehensions. 'Not exactly. They're on to us, Jonah.'

'They?'

'The school.'

He went silent for a while, but I could hear his tense breathing.

I told him about the meeting with Mrs. Foster. 'Justine must have told her,' I concluded.

'I am sorry to have put you in this predicament Phoebe. I have often feared this day would come.'

'I am sorry too, Jonah. I don't want you getting in trouble. We just need to be more careful in future.'

He sighed ruefully. 'Yes, I guess so.'

'Perhaps we should avoid meeting at school, just see each other after-hours.'

He took his time responding.

'Jonah?'

'Yes, sorry, I am here. You are right, Phoebe. It is not safe to meet on campus anymore.'

It was my turn to sigh. 'I have to go to bed now, Jonah. I will see you tomorrow… at a distance.'

'Good night… Phoebe.'

Chapter Eighteen

Diary extract dated Sunday 8th July 2001

I needed to blink several times this morning before I realised that I was actually awake and that the young man with movie star good looks staring down upon my naked body, only half covered by the quilt, was real.

He smiled lewdly, then exclaimed, 'Way to go Dad!'

I sat up with a start, gripping the quilt to my chest.

It was mid-year school break and I would be staying with Dad for the first week, so in the meantime, I was spending as much time as I could with Mr. Collins. I slept over at his house on the first Saturday night after a date with Nick.

The next morning, I received my rude awakening. Mr. Collins sat up in bed the moment that young man spoke. 'Heath, what are you doing—'

Then an approaching woman's voice shouted, '*Jonah?* What's going on? Why didn't you answer….' She stormed into the doorway of the bedroom, revealing a tall, commanding woman who was impeccably dressed. It was hard to determine her age by her perfect skin, but her assertive demeanour suggested late thirties, early forties. She looked at me, puzzled at first; then disgust overcame her as she shouted at Mr. Collins, '*Jonah! You pig!*' She stepped back outside the room. 'Put some clothes on and get your depraved arse downstairs—*pronto!*'

He glanced at me apologetically before jumping out of bed and slipping into his pants, which were amongst the mess of clothes strewn on the floor. He ran downstairs, leaving me in a state of shock with a strange guy still smiling at me.

The young man, who I had figured to be Heath, son of Mr. Collins, had golden coloured, medium length, textured hair and brown eyes blazing with passion. 'Sorry about Mum. She has the foulest of tempers.'

We could hear most of the argument that was taking place downstairs. '*How dare you barge in on me like that, Sandra!*' That was the first time I had ever heard Mr. Collins raise his voice in anger.

'*Heath was worried when you failed to answer the door, so he let himself in and I followed. It's not my fault he found… that!*'

Heath reached a hand towards me. 'Hi, I'm Heath.

Pleased to make your acquaintance.'

I took his hand to shake it, the quilt dropping to expose one breast. I quickly covered up again, blushing as I replied, 'Hi Heath. I'm Phoebe.'

The shouting continued, '*How old is she, Jonah? Is she legal? She looks young enough to be your daughter!*'

'*Yes, she is legal! What do you take me for? I may have been stupid enough to marry you, but I am not a paedophile!*'

'*Well this is hardly appropriate behaviour to demonstrate to our son, now is it?*'

I looked back from the door to Heath. 'Um, Heath?'

'Yes Phoebe?'

'Would you mind turning around so I can get dressed, please?'

He hesitated. 'Certainly…. Sorry.'

When he turned, I put my clothing on, only noticing at the end that he had been watching me in the full-length mirror the whole time. *My God! This, young man was even more lecherous than his father! Shameless too!*

'How old are you Heath?'

'Seventeen, but almost eighteen. Why do you ask?'

'Just curious.'

He grinned, then asked, 'How old are you, *Phoebe*?' He said my name in the most sexually provocative—yet without being corny—voice I had ever heard.

Before I could respond his mother cried, '*Heath, we are leaving! Come on!*'

'See *you* later, Phoebe.' He left the room.

I dropped back on the edge of the bed. The opinion I formed of Heath that day was that he was Sex personified. That really was the best way I could think to describe him.

When he reached the ground-floor, I could hear him asserting his right to stay. 'I'm old enough to decide for myself now, *Mother!*'

'Fine, but you better behave yourself, young man! And don't follow your father's *shining* example!'

The door slammed, and the shouting finally ceased. I heard Mr. Collins calmly say, 'Please wait here, son.' Then he came back up the stairs and joined me on the edge of the bed. 'I am so sorry for that intrusion, Phoebe. I—'

That was when my own anger hit. 'Why didn't you tell me you were married, or that you had a son?'

'I am no longer married. We separated four years ago and finalised the divorce at the end of last year.'

'That is beside the point, Jonah! Why didn't you tell me about any of it?' I was trembling.

'I... I guess it did not seem... pertinent at the time.'

'Not *pertinent*? How is the fact that you have a son, almost the same age as me, not *pertinent*? Or the fact that you have a raving ex-wife—how could that not be *pertinent*? Do you have any other skeletons hidden away in closets that aren't *pertinent*?'

He gaped at my outburst. 'I-I don't think—'

I stood up then and walked toward the door. 'I am going home.' Stopping at the doorway without turning to look at him, I added, 'We can talk when I get back from Dad's. I need time to cool off.'

He jumped up and tried to stop me. 'Phoebe, wait! *Please*!'

I ran down the stairs, grabbed my bag, and fled. The tears began to flow as I raced to the bus stop.

ଞେଠ

The fresh country air was just what I needed to take stock of things. It always felt so revitalising to open the window of Dad's car as soon as we left the city limits.

I was silently taking in the sights when Dad spoke up. 'I can see that something is distracting you this morning. I'm not going to press you for the details, but I'd be happy to listen when you feel ready.'

'Thanks, Dad.' Not ready to talk, I left it at that. I just needed the therapy that this lush, green landscape offered.

The old, familiar estate came into view ninety minutes after I'd kissed Mum farewell. It was a grand, federation house, situated on a large property that was once a farm. Dad loved the place because it inspired his creativity, so he decommissioned the old farm equipment, and turned the grounds into an

Australian fairyland, much like the settings of his novels. As a child, I loved exploring his garden, pretending that the ornaments were real fairies, pixies, elves, unicorns, and monsters.

When my taste in literature matured, and boys become more enchanting than anything folkloric, I would often stroll about the place and fancy myself as one of Austen's heroines, but such notions just seemed puerile to me as I walked through the front garden this time. The full impact of everything that had transpired since the end of term one just hit me then, so I dropped my bags and broke down. Dad rushed to catch my fall and gripped me tight as I wept incessantly.

Once I was finally able to speak again, I took a deep breath and asked, 'Can we go inside now? I need to talk.'

'Of course. Come on.' He carried my bags with one arm and supported me with the other as we finished our trek along the pathway to the house.

With the wood fire burning and a cup of tea in hand, I began my story. I told him everything about Mr. Collins and Nick—well mostly. I left out the gaudy details because this was my dad, not Denise. He sat silently, listening to all of it, and while his face occasionally betrayed feelings of sadness and concern, he was not shocked, and he did not judge any of us.

When finished, I asked, 'What should I do, Dad?'

'A very good question, Phoebe.' He paused to sip his tea. 'I am no expert on matters of the heart. I write fantasy because I find real people too perplexing. I'm afraid your mother is more qualified in this field, though I can understand why you don't want to bring it up with her.'

I sighed. After a while he spoke again. 'As a parent, though, my best advice is to take a break with this Mr. Collins fellow until you finish school. If you really care for him, as I can see you do, protecting his secret from the school community should be paramount to your future happiness.' He paused for another sip. 'The break would also help you focus on your studies more since your final exams will be here before you know it, and to give your heart time to find its own answers.'

'Thank you, Dad.' I sat drinking in quiet contemplation.

Once we had finished, I took our cups to the sink. When I returned to my armchair, Dad expressed another concern, 'Might I suggest something for the future?'

'Go on?' I inquired.

'If and when you return to Mr. Collins, you will need to broach the topic carefully with your mother. It is likely to be a bit close-to-home for her and may touch on some painful memories.'

Hearing Dad voice such regard for Mum's feelings came as a surprise to me. While they had worked hard at remaining civil around me, they weren't exactly chummy with each other. 'Why's that?'

'Because of what happened between your mother and me.'

It seemed that he assumed I knew. I probed further, 'I don't know your history with Mum. Neither of you ever told me. What does it have to do with my situation?'

'Your mum never...?' He seemed genuinely amazed that Mum had not told me.

'No, she didn't want to influence my opinion of you,' I assured him.

'Jeez, I guess I ought to give her more credit in future. The reason our marriage ended was because I left your mother for a much younger woman when I was thirty-eight. You were three at the time. The girl I had an affair with was eighteen.'

This news did not shock me then as it might have a little over three months prior. 'Ah, I see. I'll bear that in mind. Thanks for filling me in.'

I spent the rest of my time with Dad either reading, discussing books, or watching movies. It was too wintry to venture outside much. When I returned to Mum, I felt a lot better and knew what I was going to say to Mr. Collins.

Chapter Nineteen

Diary extract dated Saturday 14th July 2001

Despite feeling a strong urge to run into his arms and return to the way we were, I froze in place. I knew what I needed to say, why I had come here, so rushing in for his touch would only make it that much harder for me.

I didn't bother calling ahead. I wanted to see Mr. Collins face-to-face when I first spoke to him following the incident with his ex-wife. It was cold and wet when I buzzed the intercom, so thankfully he was home. He released the gate lock for me, and I stepped through. It felt strange entering through the front when I had grown accustomed to arriving via the garage door. It reminded me of my first visit.

Mr. Collins opened the front door and stood there expectantly. His warm smile and open posture went some way to soothing my aching heart.

I simply stood there in the rain, looking at him.

He frowned. 'Phoebe? What it is? Why do you not come in?'

I remained silent.

Heaving out a sigh, he crossed his arms. 'For crying out loud, Phoebe. Please come inside. You are soaked.'

His tone snapped me out of my trance, so I walked inside, allowing him to remove my saturated jacket. I was shivering, only partly due to the chill.

He wrapped a blanket around my shoulders and moved me to the couch. Mr. Collins was trembling slightly. 'You have me very worried Phoebe. What is the matter?'

I finally found the courage. 'Am I worth waiting for?'

'Waiting for what Phoebe? Why are you so cryptic?'

I thought for a moment, then rephrased my question, 'Do you value our relationship enough to wait?'

Realisation was dawning in his face. He replied mournfully, 'Oh, I see. You mean to wait out the school year?'

'Please answer me, Jonah. I need to know how you feel.'

'You mean a great deal to me, Phoebe. Have you not seen that in my manner, in the way you affect me?'

I was beginning to understand that when it came

to relationships, he saw more value in actions than words. 'I guess so, but I need to hear you say it sometimes.'

He smiled. 'Then hear this, dear Phoebe. My regard for you has grown more fervent over the last four years. I have watched you blossom from a young, dainty bud into a voluptuous and complex flower, both physically and mentally. Toward the beginning of last year, I became aware of a more intense desire for you, and I sensed a mutual attraction, so it took all the willpower I had to keep my hands off you. You are not like your peers, Phoebe. Your intellectual capacity and maturity are far beyond anything I have seen in any other teenager. Sometimes I even forget that you and I are not the same age.'

I sat there in amazement. It was true that I had long desired him, but I rarely allowed myself to hope that he wanted me before anything happened, nor had I suspected how much he revered my mind. I tried to answer, 'I… I…' But words failed me, so I kissed him fiercely. I sat back before letting my urges get the better of me. 'Thank you for telling me. These last few months have been very confusing and now more than ever my head and heart are in conflict.'

He lost himself in thought awhile, then something warm flickered his eyes. 'What if we schedule weekly, or even fortnightly rendezvous, rather than take a complete break? Perhaps we could make

Fridays after netball our night?'

He wasn't making this easy for me, but then... *Perhaps we didn't need a complete break.* It would be much safer if we kept our affair within the confines of his apartment. Less frequent meetings would also help me focus on my studies.

'Seems reasonable. I think I can manage weekly for now, maybe wind it back closer to exams.'

Satisfied with this resolution, I let him overwhelm my senses once again.

Chapter Twenty

'I have a surprise for you Phoebe,' Mr. Collins announced as soon as I stepped into his car after netball practice.

At first it was difficult to wait a whole school week before returning to the arms of Mr. Collins, but I was learning to curb my desires, saving most of them for Friday nights. This did mean, however, that those evenings were almost entirely physical.

My relationship with Nick, on the other hand, was progressing on a different level. We had not yet taken the physical aspect to the final stage, but a strong emotional bond was forming. We spent a lot of time talking about the performing arts, sports, politics, philosophy, and personal matters. On one such occasion, when Nick and I were sharing stories about ourselves, Nick asked, 'Do you have any embarrassing puberty stories, Phoebe?'

I thought a while on this. 'Not that I can think of. Why, do you?'

'Yes actually. I haven't told anyone this, not even Curtis, but when I was twelve, I failed to have sex with the hottest girl in school. She ridiculed me for months after that and I have not tried since.'

Biting my lip, but I tried to act normal. 'Oh wow! So, are you still a virgin?'

'Yes, Phoebe. When the time is right, I want you to be my first. You are the first girl I have been able to trust since then.'

A pang of guilt hit home. I knew he was referring to a different type of trust, but this still reminded me that I had not been entirely honest with him. I decided I was going to attempt to come clean with him. I kissed him on the forehead then began, 'I would be honoured, my dear. There is something I — ' But at that moment Nick's mum called us to dinner, so my own confession went unsaid and my courage did not return that night.

ဆာ

Soon after term three started at school, we received invitations to attend the school formal in late September. These invitations extended to our choice of guest, an easy decision for me to make. Nick literally jumped for joy when I asked him to be my date, spinning me around in a dizzying embrace before ravishing my mouth.

This was an exciting time for many of the girls at school, especially Denise, who began spending much of her spare time in dress shops and perusing catalogues. 'I can't decide whether to go for a soft pink or bright yellow dress. What do you think, Phoebs?' We were hanging out in her room when she asked this.

I was pretending to read a fashion magazine that she handed me, my thoughts elsewhere. When I looked at her, she was holding a couple of colour swatches against her face. I took my time with this because I knew it was important to her. 'Hmm, I think the yellow brings out your colour more.'

She stood up and looked in the mirror. 'Yes, I suppose it does. Is it *me* though?'

This was a much easier question to answer. 'Absolutely! It is bold and beautiful, just like you.'

She smiled and hugged me. 'Thanks, hun. I could kiss you for that.'

I laughed. 'You're welcome.'

෴

Friday nights after netball practice were working well. The routine was such that I would walk some distance down the road from school, meet Mr. Collins in his car and drive to his home from there.

One of these nights he had a surprise for me. Rather than driving back to his suburban townhouse, he drove around the corner and showed me a somewhat different apartment. 'This will be my new address soon.' He said this as we stepped into the lobby.

I looked at him and then at my surroundings in wonder. This was a private apartment building, yet it had a large open lobby much like a grand hotel, complete with reception desk and a lounge area that looked out into a small courtyard.

'I recently received my share of the divorce settlement and chose to invest in a more suitable living arrangement. It is on the fifteenth floor, come and see.'

I followed him into the lift. 'Why is there a reception desk? Is this a hotel?' I asked.

'No, it is not a hotel, although this place caters for a number of investment options, including renting out to holiday-makers, so they provide a concierge to help landlords with such arrangements. I believe the property management team is based on site too, assisting with matters of security, insurance, and so forth.'

That made even less sense to me. I knew very little of property and business matters.

'This place will be much closer to work for me as you may have noticed. It will also be closer to the city university campuses, should you end up attending them.' He winked at me.

We stepped out of the lift and walked a short way down the hall. When he opened the door, the sheer majesty of it stupefied me. The large open-plan living area overlooked much of the city through floor-to-ceiling windows, which Mr. Collins assured me were one-way glass. The view was breath-taking, especially at night when the city lights twinkled. It was a large unit, with three spacious bedrooms, two bathrooms (one with a three-person spa bath), and a sizeable kitchen with marble bench tops. There was even a balcony with a hot-tub and an alfresco dining area big enough to seat six people.

Once Mr. Collins finished giving me the tour, he embraced me. 'I should settle in by the time you graduate, so I would like to celebrate with you here afterwards.'

'It all looks and sounds like a dream,' was all I could say.

'Well for now, we must return to my other abode.'

ഗ്രര

The following week I attended Nick's school drama performance, along with Denise and Curtis. The play was *Much Ado About Nothing*, a favourite Shakespeare of mine, and Nick played the role of Benedick. This was the first time I had seen Nick in an official theatrical capacity, and I was impressed. I had figured he had talent to be setting his sights for the top acting school in the country, but when I saw him perform that night, I knew he was destined for greatness.

When the four of us went for a drink after, I volunteered my praise, 'You were fantastic Nick! You really brought Benedick to life up there. I think you have a real chance of pursuing your dream of attending NIDA.'

He smiled and thanked me but changed the subject. That was when I began to suspect something was wrong.

ℰℭ

Something else was unfolding around this time that I was not made aware of until later when Mr. Collins provided the following account for me.

During the week after my first look at the new city apartment, Sandra, the ex-wife, paid him a visit. She wanted this new property for herself, claiming that he had purchased it with her money anyway. She was still feeling very bitter about the divorce settlement, which had gone more in his favour. Apparently, the reason for their separation was the level of disdain they had developed for each other after years and years of fighting almost constantly.

When Mr. Collins returned home from work on Thursday that week, he found Sandra sitting at his dining table with a series of photographs laid out in front of her. Before he noticed the pictures, he challenged Sandra, *'How the hell did you get in here? Is Heath with you?'*

'Heath is at home. I *borrowed* his key.'

Then his eyes caught sight of the photos and his heart sank. He slumped into a chair and took stock of the details. There was one of me in my school sports uniform getting into his car, one of me still in uniform kissing him in his townhouse, one of me standing naked in front of him, and finally one of me riding him on the couch. 'I assume these are just copies?'

'How very astute of you, Jonah. I already have a set of prints ready to send to your workplace. You can keep these if you like.'

Resting his head in his hands, he swore under his breath. 'What do you want?'

'You already know I want that new property, but I will give you six months to sign it over to me. In the meantime, you can keep me quiet with weekly instalments of one hundred dollars, paid into this account.' She handed him the bank details, then left.

He considered calling me about it straight away but decided he didn't want to add to my stresses at the time. What was the point of cooling things off further when Sandra had all the evidence she needed? He decided that his best approach was to placate her with the weekly deposits while he worked on a plan to stop her.

Chapter Twenty-One

Diary extract dated Thursday 23rd August 2001

Just like that, it's over...

I found the application and audition information sitting on Nick's desk when I was waiting for him to return from the bathroom.

'What are you doing?' he asked.

I jumped at first, startled by his sudden return. 'I just noticed these when I glanced at your desk. This is exciting, Nick! A chance to follow your dreams. What monologue will you choose?'

He moved in close and snatched the papers from me, shoving them in his desk drawer. 'I'm not going to audition.'

I stared at him aghast. 'What? Why not?'

'Because I don't want to leave this city. I want to stay with you.'

I sunk down on his bed, feeling both flattered and horrified. 'You can't give up your life-long dream for me, Nick.'

He sat down close beside me. 'Why not? What if my dreams have changed because of you, Phoebe?'

I could not believe what I was hearing. 'How is that possible? We have only been together for a few months. We haven't even had sex yet!'

'How should that matter? Your friendship means more to me than sex. I know what my heart wants Phoebe, but now I am beginning to wonder if you even care.'

My jaw dropped at this, then I snapped, '*Of course I care!* I just don't understand how —'

'Do you though, Phoebe? Why would you want me to up and leave if you cared? I can see now why you always prioritise your studies over seeing me!'

I stood up then, feeling tears trying to push their way through, but I stood my ground. '*That's not fair Nick!* If you can't see the sense in planning for the future, then maybe we just aren't right for each other.'

'Maybe you are right Phoebe. There is no logic in what I feel, and if you can't concede that there are times when the heart should rule the head, we really aren't right for each other!'

'Fine then. Goodbye, Nick!' I stormed out of his room and didn't stop running until I was home. Once I reached my destination, I dashed to my room, and slammed the door. Dropping to my bed, I let grief engulf me.

Mum came to check on me and when she saw the

state I was in, she did not pry; she simply sat down and let me curl up in her lap as I continued to cry.

༄༅

I did not want to go to school the next day, so Mum rang the school for me to tell them I was sick. She tried to get leave from work, but I insisted she go because I wanted to be alone for a while. With reluctance, she complied. I just needed to sleep after struggling with it so much the night before.

At recess time a call from Mr. Collins woke me. 'Hello Phoebe? How are you feeling? What ails you?'

I barely had the energy to talk. 'I broke up with Nick last night.'

There was a short silence at the other end, then he continued, 'I am sorry Phoebe. I guess you must have become very close for it to affect you so. Is there anything I can do?'

'No. I just need to be alone for now, sorry.'

'I understand. Will I see you tonight?'

I thought on this a moment. I knew that both Mum and Denise would want to talk to me about it, but then his arms might be just the therapy I needed. 'Yes, I would like that. Can you pick me up at nine?'

'Okay Phoebe. Please rest well until then.'

'Yes, I will. Bye.' I hung up and went back to sleep.

At lunchtime, the phone woke me again. This time it was Denise. 'Hi Phoebs. I just got a call from Curtis. He told me you and Nick broke up. Is it true?'

Groggily I replied, 'Yes Denise. It's true.'

'Oh my God babe, I am sooo sorry! I will be round straight after school, okies?'

'Okay.'

'Hang in there, alright hun?'

'Okay.' Then I hung up and fell back to sleep.

৪৩০৪

I eventually woke up and fixed myself a snack at around four in the afternoon, which was just before Denise arrived. I was still in my pyjamas when I let her in.

'Oh wow, you look terrible hun!'

'Gee *thanks* Denise.' Sarcasm was the only tone I could muster.

She hugged me, then we sat in the loungeroom where I told her about the argument with Nick.

'Oh Phoebs. I can see you care about him lots. It's just a pity he can't see it himself.'

'Humph.'

We both sat in silence a while, then Denise exclaimed, 'Why not go to Sydney with him?'

This had not even crossed my mind. 'I don't know, Denise. It would be a big upheaval for me and —'

'Listen hun, if you really want to see Nick succeed *and* you want to be with him, then it is the best option. I'm sure there are universities in Sydney offering the courses you want to do. It'd be such an exciting place to live, too.'

I wasn't sure that I needed any more excitement in life, but I knew she was well-meaning. I tried to smile. 'I'll think on it. Thanks Denise.'

After telling Mum that I was calling it a night, at half past eight, I slipped out of my bedroom window just before nine and snuck down the street to meet Mr. Collins. He was waiting in our usual spot.

When I sat down in the car he asked, 'How are you feeling now, Phoebe?'

'Tired and miserable.'

'I see. I hope that I can bring you some comfort tonight.' He started driving.

He was slow and gentle that night. None of the intense fiery passion that was common to our meetings. This time his focus was entirely on me and my emotional needs.

I sent Nick a text message the next day, I'M SORRY, NICK. I FEEL LOUSY. PLEASE FORGIVE ME.

A prompt reply came, UR FORGIVEN. WILL TALK LATER.

This gave me some hope at least.

Chapter Twenty-Two

Diary extract dated Sunday 26th August 2001

The shocking news came over the radio around noon today. Denise and I were listening to her favourite R&B and Pop music station when they broadcast the announcement:

'Tragic news just in from the United States, where reports have revealed that 22-year-old singer and actress, Aaliyah Dana Haughton, has been found dead following a plane crash in the Bahamas...'

Denise and I looked at each other in complete and utter shock. *Aaliyah dead?* We could barely believe what we were hearing. Denise turned the radio up so that we could hear it better. Several other singers and actors were making statements about their grief at the loss of such a wonderful and talented person. We were both tearing up as we heard the words, then the radio cut to her song *I Miss You*, and we let it all out.

Shortly after they started playing a second song, Denise got a call. She was sobbing in between replies. 'Hi Curtis... Yes, we just heard... Yes, she is here...'

My ears pricked up at the obvious mention of me.

'You would...? You are the best... Love you too, babe.' She hung up, then looked at me. 'Curtis is coming over. He is bringing chocolate—oh, and Nick.'

I smiled a little at her choice of wording. We hugged and comforted each other in the meantime.

When the guys arrived, Nick came straight to me and engulfed me in his arms. 'I am so sorry, Phoebe.'

My crying resumed for a while. When I calmed down, I whispered to him, 'If you have to go to Sydney, I might be able to come with you.'

He seemed happy with that and kissed me tenderly.

That night a tribute to Aaliyah was playing on the radio, so we invited a few girls from school who were fans to Denise's house and held our own private vigil. Nick and Curtis stayed with us too, providing much needed support.

I was still finding it hard to process the news. Aaliyah became my favourite singer when I heard *One in a Million* back in Year Seven. From then on, I collected her entire discography, which included her earlier debut album and all EPs. *Age Ain't Nothing but a Number* truly resonated with me that year and I would often play it in the months following my first time with Mr. Collins. Her voice was incredibly smooth and sexy, and her songs provided insights into relationships that I was only just beginning to grasp myself that year. It was tragic that her life had been cut so short.

Chapter Twenty-Three

Diary extract dated Friday 21ˢᵗ September 2001

He beckoned me toward the bed, where he slowly undressed me, starting with the zip of my dress. He pulled the straps off my shoulders and let the mass of burgundy chiffon fall to the floor. When he caught sight of my corset, he sat back and admired the view for a moment. He fumbled a bit when trying to undo all the hooks and then got a little baffled by the way the suspender straps attached to my stockings, so I helped him with those.

Once my own disrobing was complete, I knelt on the edge of the bed to remove Nick's clothing. His hunger for me became more obvious with every layer I shed.

The school formal was fast approaching, and I still did not have a dress picked out—much to Denise's horror—so she insisted on taking me shopping.

Following my reunion with Nick, I confirmed that he still wanted to be my formal date. His response was one of excited enthusiasm and he decided then that he wanted to book a hotel room for us to retire to afterwards. He did not say anything about his intentions, but I figured it would be the night.

Denise supported my speculations when I told her about these plans at the dress shop. 'Oh my God babe, it is so obvious what he wants to do! We are definitely gonna have to take you lingerie shopping after this!'

I smiled and acted bashful. We continued to look at dresses and I eventually found a burgundy spaghetti-strap dress that I fell in love with. '*Yes!* This is perfect!' I exclaimed. It was a long, A-line, chiffon number with a split in the skirt that started half-way down my thigh. The neckline was more revealing than my usual style, but I was beginning to feel more adventurous, and Denise approved of my choice, so it was settled.

We moved on to the intimate apparel section next, which was when Denise started to offer up advice from her own sexual experiences. 'I know a lot of girls have complained that their first time hurt, but mine didn't. I think it can have a lot to do with how well the guy prepares you for it.'

'Do you mean foreplay?' I played along because I didn't want to let on about my own. Such a revelation was sure to arouse suspicions.

'Yes exactly. Make sure Nick knows about this too, because I doubt he would want to hurt you.'

I thought about my first time. I didn't recall pain, even without much prep-work. *Perhaps the anticipation was enough.* I showed Denise a lace burgundy corset. 'What do you think?'

'Looks like a good match for your dress. Better check that it sits ok underneath though.'

I put it in a basket with some other items to try on.

'Some guys can finish pretty quickly too, especially if it is their first time, or it has been a while since they got any. If this happens, try not to act disappointed if you don't want to hurt Nick's feelings.'

Good point, especially in Nick's case. I was holding up a black chiffon negligee at this point.

Denise nodded approvingly. 'If the guy is really into you, which Nick obviously is, he will probably be willing to go a second time and sometimes even a third in one night, so you might still get off then.'

Oh wow — were there times she went without orgasms? Bonus points for Mr. Collins! We found a clearance sale bin just then and my basket started filling up quickly.

'Just be mindful of the recovery time. This is different for every guy and even the same guy can have different rates-of-return.'

My God — she sounded so business-like talking about it! Was that what sex had become for her?

'But you can always use this recovery time to make out more, rest a while, or even watch a movie. Erotic films are usually best if you do this though.'

'You mean Porn?'

'Well not all erotic films are porn. A lot of them have complex plotlines. Porn is still fine though. It often gets the best results in my experience, because the plot doesn't become a distraction.' She grinned.

With two baskets overflowing, I decided to make my way to the changerooms. When I left the store, I had enough new underwear to entirely replace the existing content in my drawers.

&⊃&⊃

According to Mr. Collins, the day I spent shopping was when he hired a Private Investigator. He'd sought legal advice on the matter of Sandra's blackmail a few weeks earlier and was sure he could build a case against her, but he needed to produce substantial evidence of her extortion. This was what led to the PI. I didn't even know this was something that happened for real in Australia. I thought Private Eyes were mostly the stuff of books, movies and television dramas; I just assumed that any real ones would be based in the big cities of foreign countries.

&⊃&⊃

The Year Twelve Dinner Dance was upon us. Denise

hired a limo—a bit extravagant I thought—but I knew she placed a lot more importance on this night than any other girl in the school.

Denise had, of course, been part of the planning committee, so thanks to the intel she willingly shared with me in the lead up, I knew exactly who we would be sitting with. As a result of previous classes behaving badly during the dinner, teachers needed to supervise each table. A lot of the students thought this was a drag, but when Denise told me she had picked Mr. Collins to join our table, I was far from disappointed. She had failed, however, to inform me that he would sit directly next to me. I wondered if this part of the arrangement was her doing, or his.

Mr. Collins greeted us all, although I noticed his eyes drawn to me the most. 'Good evening, ladies, gentlemen. You all look very charming tonight.'

We found our places at our tables, where we were expected to remain standing behind our chairs while Mrs. Caldwell addressed us all with a welcome speech. We were then required to join hands with our neighbours to say a prayer of thanks. Mr. Collins gripped my hand tightly, more so than Nick.

When it was time to be seated, Nick pulled my chair out to assist me in a gentlemanly fashion and I could see Curtis did the same for Denise.

During the meal, Nick spent much time talking to Mr. Collins, easing the tension I felt at the start of the night.

Between our main course and dessert, I had my hands sitting in my lap when I felt Mr. Collins slip something into them. I remained nonchalant and put it in my bag, taking it for a trip to the ladies' room. When I reached the bathroom, I inspected the item and found a hotel room key card wrapped inside a note.

> Room 619, this Hotel. Please join me later. If you cannot meet me, for whatever reason, please respond by returning the key.

I decided that I would pay him a visit that night, once Nick was asleep, so I kept the key and sent him a text: I WILL JOIN YOU, BUT IT'LL BE VERY LATE.

The formal proceedings continued until around ten o'clock, during which time we all had a lot of fun dancing—well most of us. I noticed that Mr. Collins was not keen on dancing, but he seemed to enjoy watching.

Some of the girls invited Nick and me to an after-party, but Nick pretended he felt tired, so I followed suit and we bee-lined for the hotel room he'd booked. As soon as we were in the lift, he grabbed me and kissed me with more fervour than ever before.

When we reached the sixth floor, the lift stopped, so he paused long enough to lead me down the corridor. I couldn't help but notice that room 619 was directly opposite our own. *Was this a coincidence?*

Once inside the room, Nick made straight for the bedside tables where he turned on a stereo that softly played some of our favourite dance music and lit some candles. He turned off the electric lights, then resumed kissing me. Once we were both naked, I laid back on the bed, allowing Nick to take his time preparing me. I was most definitely ready for him when it finally happened, and it happened three times.

℘ℭ℘

It was around two in the morning when I was sure that Nick was sound asleep. I slipped back into my clothes, although I left my shoes off, grabbed his key card, and snuck across the hall. Mr. Collins was sitting up in bed, reading a book, when I entered.

He looked up at me, noticing that I was not entirely dressed. 'Am I to infer that you did not venture far to get here?'

'A safe assumption, I am sure.' I stood before him and removed my dress, revealing the corset with suspenders holding up my sheer stockings.

His intake of breath was beyond obvious. He moved to the edge of the bed where he could reach me, and began to unclip my straps as he spoke, 'Very nice. I would love to see you in more garments like these…. They imply a greater level of maturity in their wearer.' Then he moved his hands to undo my corset, kissing me as he did so.

He pinned my naked body to the bed and looked into my eyes avidly as he spoke. 'Now Phoebe, I want you to tell me everything that transpired between you and Nick in that hotel room tonight.'

Um, what? 'You really want to know about that *now*?'

He started to caress my left nipple with his tongue. 'Yes, now is exactly when I want to know.'

This was the strangest type of foreplay!

'Well first he set a very romantic atmosphere with soft music and candles, then he took his time stimulating me.' I paused to gauge his reaction.

'Go on.' His teeth gently gripped my nipple.

I started to squirm from the thrill of his touch. 'Then he penetrated me, but he was slow and gentle.'

'Gentle you say?' Those teeth bit down a little, but not enough to hurt.

I groaned loudly. 'Yes, it felt very different to sex with you.'

His mouth moved across to my other nipple. 'Did you enjoy it?'

'Yes, very much. But—'

He sucked it hard and I groaned again. 'But what?'

'It didn't feel as good as it does with you.'

He looked at me then and smiled. 'Is that so?' He didn't give me an opportunity to answer.

ౠ⭑

I did not return to Nick's bed until around half past five that morning, by which time I collapsed from exhaustion.

Waking to the feel of Nick gently kissing the back of my neck and shoulders, I yawned. 'Mm last night was incredible.'

At the sound of my voice he pulled me over so that I was on my back. 'I'm so glad to hear you say that.' He kissed my mouth, then took me again.

Chapter Twenty-Four

Diary extract dated Friday 12th October 2001

I could hear voices at my door, then it swung open. We barely had enough warning to release our hold of each other. Both Mum and Nick entered the room, with Mum proclaiming, 'Ah there you are! Nick and I have been looking everywhere for you! It's cake time!'

Nick looked at the two of eyes narrowing in on our proximity.

I moved over to Nick and quickly responded, 'Sorry Mum, I was just showing Mr. Collins my library.'

Nick grabbed my hand, still looking at Jonah warily, then led me back to the family room.

The mid-semester break was always a busy time of year in the Braddock household. After a while we began to call it the Spring

Party Season. This was because both Mum and I had our birthdays close together, along with some of Mum's cousins. It was also a popular time for family weddings, christenings, baby showers, bridal showers, etc. etc. Thankfully, I needed to worry about two gatherings this spring. Mum understood my study needs, so she excused me from many of the other functions.

Mum's birthday came on the 30th September and we celebrated with an afternoon tea in the garden. This did not mean that she would skimp on the catering by any means. When Laura Braddock hosted anything, she spent weeks baking and a small fortune on drinks and decorations.

She personally invited Nick to her party, having become good friends with him, and during the day he observed, 'Jonah's not here. I would have expected to see him today.'

Mum looked puzzled by this. His remark confused me at first, then I remembered my stupid lie when I first introduced them. I guess it was time to dig myself back out of that hole. I just hoped I didn't end up deeper.

'Oh, well Mr. Collins couldn't make it.' Then I tactfully changed the subject.

Later that night, when most of the guests had gone, and Nick was in the bathroom, I asked Mum, 'Is it okay if I invite Mr. Collins to my Birthday? He is a good friend of Nick's, and he is my favourite teacher.'

'Of course, dear. It's your birthday.'

ഇൗ

I turned nineteen on the 12th October, and the festivities Mum held in my honour took place that night. Decorations filled multiple rooms across the house, showcasing the black and gold colour scheme, and a marquee with a dancefloor stood on the back lawn. It was almost as grand as my eighteenth birthday, just without the jukebox and disco lights. This time Nick volunteered to take care of the music playlist for me, and he did not disappoint.

I told Mr. Collins that Nick would be under the assumption that most of my family knew him as Jonah, so he should make a point of mingling with them. I think this made him a bit anxious. 'I am not so sure that my attendance is a good idea.'

I smiled at him reassuringly. 'You will be fine. Just act natural and let your British charm take care of the rest.'

Mr. Collins was well received by my family that night. In fact, something Mum said even startled me a little. She approached me in the kitchen, where Denise and I were mixing some drinks, and casually asked, 'Mr. Collins is very handsome; do you know if he is single?'

I lost control of my cocktail shaker, spraying the

contents all over the kitchen sink as I exclaimed, '*Mum!*'

'Well, it is only a matter of time before you fly the coop, Phoebe, so I'm dusting off the cobwebs and stepping back out into the dating arena.'

I avoided eye contact by focusing on the clean-up job in front of me. 'I think he is married, or at least was. He has a teenage son.'

'I guess I will have to ask him myself.' She strode off back to the throng.

Denise giggled; adding insult to injury, 'Oh wow—your mum with Mr. Collins would be pretty funny.'

I simply glared at her.

For the next two hours my eyes constantly diverted to the spectacle that was Mum flirting with Mr. Collins. While the attention was not entirely welcome, he took it in his stride. When Mum's catering duties preoccupied her, Mr. Collins took advantage of his freedom and escaped down the hall to the first door on the left. I was in the family room at the time, so I stealthily excused myself from the group and followed him.

Looking at my book collection when I found him, he did not turn his head as I entered the room. 'You have an extraordinary array of antiquities here, Phoebe.'

'Thank you, Jonah. I have been collecting since I was twelve.' I drew up close to him and brushed his hand with mine. 'Sorry about my Mum.'

He turned to me and smiled. 'Oh, she is harmless. I will confess that her attentions flattered me at first, but I will set things straight before the end of the night.' Putting his arm around my waist, he pulled me in close, and kissed me.

We must have been kissing for a considerable time, based on the intrusion that followed. I hoped Nick would forget about it before the night was through.

Once the obligatory humiliation of listening to an off-key crowd sing to me finally finished, I blew out the candles on my cake.

Two remained alight, so of course Denise joked, 'Apparently you have two boyfriends, Phoebs!'

I struggled to laugh it off. 'That's so ridiculous, Denise! I can't believe you remember that silly old tradition.' When I chanced a glance at Mr. Collins, his expression gleamed.

The gift giving came after the cake cutting. Firstly, my extended family inundated me with a range of vouchers, unable to bring themselves to give cash, but having no idea what I wanted or needed.

Mum gave me a bottle of my favourite perfume, which was running low. 'Happy birthday, sweetheart.'

'Thank you, Mum, I definitely need more of this.'

I almost cried when I opened the parcel Denise handed me. It was a framed poster of Aaliyah, complete with her autograph. 'Oh my God, hun. I don't even….' I stood and hugged her tight.

Next up, Mr. Collins sauntered over. I really wasn't expecting anything from him, so he surprised me with a wrapped box. 'It is a book… You can open it later.'

I could detect some subtle inference in his tone, so I put it aside and thanked him. I felt somewhat glad I'd waited because when I opened that box, I found a first edition Complete Works of John Wilmot, Earl of Rochester, who I knew to be a libertine. Anyone else who knew this would have considered such a gift from one's English teacher to be highly inappropriate. I later thanked him in a most inappropriate way.

Nick approached me last, handing me a small box carrying far more weight than anything else I received that day. I opened it to find a promise ring with an engraving that read "My Dear." It rendered me speechless for a moment as I teared up. Then I embraced him and quietly whispered, 'Thank you, Nick, my dear.'

'You are welcome, Phoebe, my dear.'

The party grew lively again for several more hours, although most of my extended family had left. Mr. Collins also bid us farewell since the night was turning into more of a dance party.

Chapter Twenty-Five

Diary extract dated Saturday 24th November 2001

Christmas Gift List for 2001:

*Mum-A new summer hat and beach towel

*Dad-Bottle of Port

*Jonah-A rare book

*Nick-The latest Ministry of Sound CD and The Moulin Rouge DVD

*Denise-A perfume sampler pack and 100% Hits: The Best of 2001 + Summer Hits CD

*Curtis-PlayStation 2 Game

*Other School Friends-charm bracelet charms.

*Grandparents-Fancy soaps.

*Aunts & Uncles-Bottles of Wine

*Cousins-Chocolates

The last of my school days were so close I could almost reach out and touch them. We no longer had any contact time at school because exams took up most of the term. Thankfully, I only had a couple of exams and the rest of the work I needed to do was assignment-based, which I finish easily enough.

During the final week of term three, we were given information about our graduation, including a request to book our tickets for the ceremony and dinner-dance. I invited Nick to attend, but he regretfully declined because his own was on the same night.

'That is so frustrating! Why would they do that when they know so many of the girls from your school date guys at my school!' he said.

'Maybe that was the only time they could schedule it. I don't know. It still sucks though.'

His frown turned to a grin as he remembered something. 'If you join me at schoolies, I will make it up to you.'

I sighed. 'I don't know Nick. I've heard bad things about schoolies. Can I think on it?'

'I assure you that we have booked our own private holiday house, so it would just be Curtis, Denise, and us lodging together, and we don't have to go to the unsanctioned events.'

'I'll think about it.'

ℰℭ

With study out the way, I took some time to shop for my last ever school formal dress. I asked Mum to take me since she had worked hard to get me through school. It also gave us some quality bonding time which we had both been missing while my end of year work absorbed much of my time.

We browsed countless stores, looking at lots of dresses, but none of them seemed right. They were either too subdued for my grand event, or they just didn't look good on me. At least this gave us plenty of time to talk. As I was walking out of a changeroom, I broached the topic of Nick, 'Can I ask you something, Mum?'

'Of course, sweetie. What is it?'

I put the latest lot of dresses that were no good back on the returns rack. 'There is a strong chance that Nick will be offered a really good study opportunity in Sydney next year, but he said he would only go if I went with him. I said I might go, but to be honest, I'm not sure what to do. Should I go?'

'Oh, sweetheart, there are some serious decisions to make here. I can see that Nick cares for you a great deal and I would be quite happy for you to move in with him when you are ready, but moving interstate is a big deal and warrants a lot of considerations.'

We were walking into another store at this point.

'What do you mean?' I asked.

'Firstly, do you have any other reasons to move there yourself, or would it just be for his sake?'

'I have looked into university options over there and they have some really good courses that I would be happy to study. It would also be fun and exciting to live in such a big city.' I held a green dress up against myself for Mum's opinion.

She dismissed it straight away. 'Such a big move is sure to be stressful. Have the two of you worked through issues much before?'

'No, not really. The only issue was that minor breakup we had over him auditioning in the first place.' She held up a long, navy-blue dress. I shook my head and we moved on. 'Are you suggesting that it isn't a good idea to move?'

'Not at all. I think it would be a great opportunity for you both, but you need to spend some time looking at it from all angles. A very important question to ask yourself is whether you feel strongly enough for him. If your heart isn't one hundred percent in the relationship, then it would be unwise to go unless you prepared yourself for living alone.'

'Okay, thanks Mum.' This gave me some good food for thought and I left it there.

Then we found it, the perfect garment. Mum and I both gasped when we saw it. 'It is absolutely gorgeous, hun. You must try this on!'

What I found was a strapless, mermaid-style dress

with a pink to red hombre shade covered in glittering crystals. Then I looked at the price-tag and my heart sank. 'It's extremely expensive Mum.'

She smiled. 'Don't worry about that, Phoebe. Let me take care of the cost. I think it is a fair bet that you will only graduate from high school once.'

'You are the best Mum! I will try it on. I just hope it fits okay!' I was ecstatic that it fit perfectly! Only accessorising remained.

෨෬

Denise turned eighteen on Wednesday 21st, but due to exams we had to wait until the weekend to celebrate. I insisted on planning this one, with some financial help from her parents, because I wanted my best friend to have the most fun and memorable of parties. I booked out a private function room in an upper-class hotel in the city and got the girls to chip in for a bar tab. I also hired a good DJ to take care of the music, ensuring he included all her favourites.

I took her shopping the night before the party because I wanted to purchase a dress as part of my gift to her. We found her a stunning white designer label that hugged her chest and hips then flared out around the knees. She was ecstatic when we got it. 'Oh my God Phoebs! You are the best! But wait... are you sure you can afford it?' She was looking at the price tag when she asked this.

'I have been saving especially for this event hun,

so yes, I can afford it.'

Denise squealed and hugged me in response.

I also took this opportunity to sort my own outfit. I went with a knee-length black dress from the same designer that was on a discount rack for some minor defect that I couldn't see. This one was an asymmetrical off-the-shoulder number that was figure hugging all over, with corset lacing along one of the side seams.

The party itself was perfect. Denise had a blast, surrounded by all her friends and close family, dancing to her favourite music. It was good to see her in her element.

When it came time for speeches, I grabbed Denise and led her up to the microphone. I started with a few of my own words, reading from some written notes: 'Ladies and Gentlemen, thank you all for joining us tonight to celebrate this momentous occasion. I am honoured to be standing alongside my best friend, Denise, on this night when we mark her coming of age. I will never forget that fateful day, at the start of year two, when this bubbly young girl walked into my classroom and bee-lined for the seat next to mine, and without any pretence, she announced "You are pretty, I think I will sit with you!"'

This got a few laughs from the crowd as well as Denise. I went on, 'I replied with "Um Hi." Some of you might find this hard to believe, but I was very shy and quiet back then, so I didn't really know how else to respond.' A few more laughs.

'From that day forward, the two of us were inseparable. I don't know what I would have done without this girl. Denise taught me everything I know about fashion and makeup, but more importantly, she has shown me the value of true friendship. She has helped a few of us come out of our shells and she has supported me through some of the most difficult times in my life.'

Denise started to tear up at this point, the very trigger for my own tears. The rest of my speech became much harder to voice. 'Denise... you are... the most gregarious and talkative person I know... you are also... kind, thoughtful... and generous. You... are... an inspiration to all... who cross your path.' We were both openly weeping at this point. 'I would like to call a toast... Ladies and Gentlemen... please raise your glasses.' I raised my own champagne flute. 'Cheers to this beautiful woman. Happy birthday Denise!'

A resounding "Happy birthday Denise" filled the room. Then I handed the microphone to Denise who spoke, 'Thanks, Phoebs, you are a gem! Wow, um, I think I'm like speechless for the first time ever.' We all laughed, giving her enough encouragement to continue. 'Thanks everyone for coming. I love you all!' She paused as everyone cheered. 'I would especially like to thank a few of you. Thanks again to my bestie, Phoebe. That was the most touching speech in the history of speeches! You have also done an amazing job organising this event. Can we all give it up for Phoebe Braddock!'

They all clapped and cheered for me. I blushed and graciously accepted their praise, after which, I shrank back into the crowd where Nick's arms enfolded me. He whispered softly in my ear, 'You are a marvel, my dear.'

Denise continued her speech. 'I also want to thank Mum and Dad. You guys are awesome parents! Thank you so much for putting up with me for eighteen years!'

Dana and Mark both responded together, 'You're welcome (sweetie). Love you.'

Denise grabbed Curtis then, dragging him into the limelight. 'I also want to thank this man. My gorgeous boyfriend. Curtis has been a wonderful support for me this year.' Turning to him she added, 'I love you babe.' Then she kissed him, and we all cheered.

At midnight, the venue was closing, but most of us wanted to keep going, so Denise suggested a night club. 'Hey Phoebs, what's that club you and Nick love going to?'

'The Vault?' I offered.

She clapped her hands. 'That's it! Let's go there!'

This decision thrilled both Nick and me, and I was excited to show it off to my best friend.

Denise gaped as we stepped inside. 'Wow this place is a-*mazing*!' She hugged me tight. 'Thanks so much hun! This has been *the* best night!'

I beamed with delight.

၈၁၄

It was only in Christmas shopping that my excitement over retail outstripped Denise's. I think this was partly due to my love of all things Christmas, but mostly because I enjoyed spending time thinking about the people in my life and what they would appreciate receiving. Denise was much less confident in her choices, insisting on going with me every year so that she could seek my advice. This year my list was bigger than ever, and I was itching to get out to the shops to find the perfect gift for everyone. The First Weekend of December was our traditional time and the mall was buzzing with the sights and sounds of the festive season.

'Phoebs? I was thinking of getting Curtis tickets to either the Australian Open, or the Grand Prix. What do you think?'

I gave this some thought before replying, 'I would go for the Grand Prix. It sounds more exciting in my opinion; and I know Curtis would love both options.'

'Perfect! Thanks, hun. That's one item sorted.' She made a note on her shopping list, then looked up smiling. 'So, what are you getting for Nick?'

'I was thinking of getting him the latest *Ministry of*

Sound CD and the *Moulin Rouge* DVD.'

'That's a great idea! Let's get to it.'

We started in the Hi-Fi store, where I was able to get Nick's gift, although the DVD wasn't out yet, so I pre-ordered it. I also picked up a PlayStation 2 game for Curtis and stealthily found a CD for Denise whilst we were there.

As we left this shop, Denise linked arms with me. 'Bummer about that DVD, I hope it comes in on time for you.'

'Yeh, me too.'

'Where to next?'

We both looked at our lists, then in unison exclaimed, 'Jewellery store!'

Denise declared, 'Jinx!'

And we both laughed. It had become a tradition for us to both go in on the same gifts for our school friends. These would always be charms for the bracelets that we got them in year eight. 'These graduation hats would be an ideal charm,' I suggested.

Denise nodded approvingly as she started to tear up.

'What is it hun?' I asked.

'I can't believe school's over! We probably won't see most of our friends much anymore, and if you... go to Sydney...'

I hugged her, feeling my own tears rising to the surface. The jeweller even gave us a sympathetic smile. 'I know hun. It's gonna be tough. I promise to call you lots and see you as often as possible, no matter where I end up.'

'Thanks, Phoebs,' she sobbed.

After finalising our purchase of ten graduation hat charms, I put forward an idea, 'I know what might cheer us up. Let's forget our age and this whole growing up business for a bit and go visit Santa!'

Denise giggled. 'I think we will make his day too.'

We put our shopping in Denise's car, then made our way to Santa's cave. We got some strange looks from the parents during the line-up but shrugged it off. When we were finally called in to see the jolly fat man, he let out a cheerful chuckle. 'Well ladies, I must say I'm surprised to see girls of your age here.'

We both took a seat on each of his knees and I greeted him. 'Hi Santa, I'm Phoebe. My friend, Denise here, needed some cheering up. I figured seeing you would help.'

'I see. Tell me, Denise, what's got you feeling glum?'

'We are finishing High School and I'm sad to be leaving all my friends,' she replied.

He looked thoughtful for a moment, then went on. 'Ah yes, that is a difficult time. Change can be hard for all of us, but it is also good. I'm sure that wherever you both end up; you will make lots of new friends. And I happen to know that the *really* good ones will grow with you, no matter what happens.'

This made Denise smile. 'Thanks, Santa.'

'Yes, thank you for your words of wisdom,' I added.

He chuckled again, then replied, 'Ah no worries. Now tell me ladies, what would you like for Christmas?'

Denise went first. 'Let me think… I'd like some more perfume, oh and I need new clothes for summer.'

He smiled. 'Very good. I'll see what I can do. Phoebe?'

I had always found this a difficult question to answer when my parents asked. 'Um… I don't really know.'

'Come on, there must be something?' he insisted.

'Well there is one thing…'

'Yes?'

I leaned in to whisper in his ear. 'The courage to be more honest with everyone.'

He looked straight at me, frowning slightly, as he replied, 'That is a tricky one, I'm afraid. Not really the sort of thing I keep in stock.'

'I know — sorry Santa. But I can't think of anything else.'

'Well in that case, I will see what I can do.'

We both stood up then.

He gave us a big grin. 'I hope you both have a very merry Christmas.'

'Thanks Santa,' Denise said.

'You too,' I added.

Then we left and continued our shopping, but we didn't get far before Denise asked, 'What did you ask Santa?'

I blushed. 'It's a little embarrassing.'

'Come on hun, this is me here. You can trust me with anything.'

I sighed. 'I asked him for courage.'

She giggled. 'Okay, that is a strange request. Have you been watching the *Wizard of Oz* again lately?'

'Maybe.'

Chapter Twenty-Six

Diary extract dated Saturday 15th December 2001

After finishing breakfast, I confronted him, 'So, I explored the apartment a bit this morning. I was excited about getting these keys you see.'

I held up the gift that he'd given me the previous night. He smiled at first.

'I assure you that I did not intend to pry into your private matters. I just wanted to familiarise myself with the place. But then I got a bit of a shock when I tested this key.' I pointed out the one for the desk.

He looked uncertain when he examined it, but then his visage changed to one of remorse as soon as he remembered what it unlocked.

G raduation night was full of mixed emotions for me. On the one hand I felt relieved to get past the hurdle of my senior studies and excited to be able to see Jonah without the fear of risking his job, but on the other hand I was sad to say goodbye to a great deal of friends who I would not see as often anymore. I also feared the great unknown that was my future.

Neither Denise nor I had dates, so when the DJ played a few slow songs we danced together. During the third of these, when Usher was singing *You Got it Bad*, I caught Jonah watching me intently and came dangerously close to forgetting who my dance partner was. Thankfully, the music changed in time, bringing us the Queens of R&B performing *Lady Marmalade*, so we re-joined the larger group to strut our stuff.

Jonah caught me alone at the bar for a moment, when I was taking a break from the dance floor, and whispered, '*Voulez vous coucher avec moi?*'

I had my own copy of the *Moulin Rouge* soundtrack, so I knew full well what he meant. I smiled. '*Oui.*'

When the function centre closed at midnight, I said farewell to Denise and the other girls, telling them that I was going to stay in a hotel room. I walked over to where I could see Jonah waiting.

He spoke quietly as soon as I was in earshot. 'The urge to grab you right now is incredibly strong. However, we must maintain some composure and walk beside each other without physical contact.'

'I understand.'

The walk back to his apartment was arduous. He was no longer my teacher, so we were free to be lovers, but I knew others would be suspicious if we jumped straight into each other's arms. This meant that every step made before reaching our destination was that much harder.

When the door of the lift closed, we could not take it any longer. He scooped me into his arms and kissed me, letting go only once the door opened on his floor. He held my hand tight as we walked up the corridor.

I was awestruck the moment Jonah opened the door. An atmosphere of pure romance had been set throughout, complete with soft jazz, candles, and paths of rose petals that started at the front door and trailed off towards the bathroom and his bedroom. He turned to me. 'Our liaison started in a very heated and passionate way, leaving little time for sentiment at first; so, I wanted to show you that romance is not a foreign concept to me.'

Then he picked me up and carried me to the bathroom. Sitting me down next to the spa, he ran the water. Then he took his time undressing me while the tub filled, kissing my body as he went. Once we were in the water, he opened a bottle of French champagne for us to toast with. 'Here is to the end of one chapter of your life, Phoebe, and to the beginning of another. Congratulations on your graduation.'

'Thank you, Jonah.'

We emptied our glasses, then let our passions take over.

After the spa, he carried me to his bedroom where I found more surprises waiting. There was box of chocolates by the bed and a small gift-wrapped parcel. He placed me on the bed, opened the chocolates, and put one in my mouth.

'Mm wow, that was delicious,' I declared as I swallowed the divine treat. 'You are overwhelming my senses tonight.'

He grinned. 'Excellent. That was my plan. Here, a little graduation gift for you.'

'You really didn't need to.'

'Please, just open it Phoebe,' Jonah insisted in a mildly anxious tone.

I don't know what I was imagining the box would hold. It was too small for a book. I might have been thinking jewellery, but what it contained was quite unexpected. It was a set of keys on a chain with a silver heart pendant. I looked at him questioningly.

'You are welcome here anytime Phoebe, whether I am home or not.' I had no words to thank him with, but then I didn't need words.

&)Q

I awoke early the next morning and the excitement of what lay before me kept me from falling back to sleep, so I decided to explore the place. First, I raided the pantry, although I was not hungry yet. I figured that I would attempt to cook breakfast a little later. I looked around in the spare rooms. A queen-sized bed and other furniture filled one, most likely for when Heath stayed over. I paused in here a moment, wondering if I would see him again that summer.

Then I moved on to the other room, which Jonah had turned into a study. Bookshelves lined the walls of this room, with the only other furniture being an old rolltop desk. I tried to open it, but found it locked. Feeling curious, I tested the keys on my new chain and found one that worked. I would have been happy to leave it at that, but a stack of papers on his desk caught my attention.

I was furious! I could not believe he had kept this from me.

I decided to prepare breakfast all the same. This incident may have been the first example of what I have come to refer to as "Rage Cooking." I was frying the last of the pancakes when I heard him enter the living area.

'That smells delightful, Phoebe. You really are a treasure.'

I added the contents of the pan to the pile and set the plate upon the table. Then I sat down silently and ate. Jonah seemed a little puzzled by my lack of affection or speech, but I used this time to carefully plan my approach.

When we finished the food, I told him about my

exploration, showing him the desk key and questioning the papers I found. I tried to stay calm. 'Why did you hide this from me for so long?'

'This matter did not need to concern you Phoebe. You were busy with your studies and it would have added unnecessary stress. I took care of it and Sandra has ceased her extortion.'

'I was in those photos, Jonah, so it totally did concern me! Besides, what right did you have to decide what stress was appropriate for me! I thought we were in this together. I should have been there to help you through this. You need to stop treating me like a child!' I was beginning to lose my cool.

'And how, pray tell, could you have helped me? This had nothing to do with our age difference, Phoebe. You did not have a law degree or skills as an investigator. That was what I needed to put an end to that woman's blackmail.'

I stared at him in disbelief. 'I would have provided emotional support, Jonah. That's what partners do, is it not?'

'I am sorry Phoebe, but when did we become *partners*? Beyond the classroom, we have only ever been lovers in a sordid affair. I may have had hopes of becoming your partner once, but the strong bond you have formed with Nick killed those hopes. *He* is your partner, not me.'

This came as a huge blow that almost knocked the wind out of me. I thought things had been progressing well for the two of us and my feelings for him were just as strong as they were for Nick. I began to tear up. 'Is that really how you feel?'

He did not voice his answer, nor did he need to. I could see the pain in his eyes.

'I have always borne a strong attachment to you, Jonah. Just because I have become close to Nick, that does not negate how I feel for you.'

'The time has come to stop messing with everyone's hearts, Phoebe. You must choose a partner. I am content to remain your lover, but I refuse to continue hiding in the shadows. So, if you want things to carry on as they are, you will have to tell Nick about us. If, on the other hand, you want me as your partner, you will need to kiss Nick goodbye.'

I had feared that this day would come. *How was I to choose between them?* 'Oh God, Jonah, this is a very difficult decision for me to make. Please give me some time to think it over.'

He sighed. 'Yes, of course. I will give you until the end of January. I know that a lot will be happening for you in these coming weeks and perhaps some of these events will influence your verdict.'

I calmed a little. 'Thank you.'

Chapter Twenty-Seven

Diary extract dated Thursday 20th December 2001

Considering how "blonde" Denise acts, I often forget how goddamned perceptive she can be. I was drunk. They ambushed me. I was never going to be able to hide it forever.

When I arrived home following my discussion with Jonah, I rang Nick. 'Hi, how are you? How was your night?'

'Hi Phoebe. I'm a bit hung-over, but I think the worst has passed. I had a great night, although I missed you terribly. How'd your grad go?'

The sound of his voice soothed me. 'My night was good, although I missed you too.'

'Have you decided what to do about schoolies?'

Until that morning I was almost certain that I wouldn't go. I had been planning to spend more time with Jonah. But then I figured a week away with Nick would give me a good opportunity to really gauge the strength of our relationship. 'You know what, I think I will come.'

'*Yes*! That is music to my ears!' Nick exclaimed down the phone line. So, we made our plans.

We drove through some stunning farmland and rolling hills on our way down to the cove, a picture of natural beauty with crystal clear blue waters and perfect white sands. Our gorgeous holiday house sat one block back from the beach. It was like a modern style provincial place with lots of windows and white furnishings. There were four bedrooms in total, although we only used two.

We spent most of the week having carefree fun and Nick made a point of carefully choosing the events we attended to set my mind at ease.

On the Thursday night we decided to stay in and have a quiet one since the following night was entailed a huge farewell party at the official schoolies club. We ended up playing a game of dirty truth-or-dare whilst drinking the last of our alcohol supplies.

The rules: all questions had to be sex related; we took turns answering a question by each other member of the group; and if we refused, or if someone believed we were lying, we had to complete a dare. Curtis volunteered to be the first interrogation subject.

I started the questioning, 'When did you lose your virginity?'

He was quick to reply, 'That's an easy one. I was fifteen.'

Denise giggled. 'I think you were the only one here that didn't know that Phoebe.'

Then Nick asked him, 'Have you ever paid for sex?'

Curtis hesitated this time, and his face turned red. 'Yes.'

'Holy shit, man, *really*?' Nick looked as shocked as I felt.

'How often?' Denise asked with wide eyes.

Again, he dithered. 'Twice.'

Nick continued his questioning, 'I'm sorry Curtis, but we're best mates and you've never told me about this before, so you gotta spill now. Like why did you, and what happened?'

There was a pained expression on Curtis' face. 'It was last year, after Amy dumped me. I was feeling pretty low about myself, and I really wanted her back. I was driving through the city late one night when I saw a hooker who looked a lot like Amy, so I hired her. She left me her number and I called her back a week later. It all felt pretty empty, and I felt like crap afterwards, so I didn't continue after the second time.'

'Ah, geez, I knew your breakup with Amy hit you hard, but I had no idea you were hurting that much. I'm sorry to have brought it up again.' Nick simpered.

Curtis forced a smile. 'Nah, it's okay. I'm in a much better place now.' His smile widened as he put his arm around Denise. Curtis had grown on me in the months following Aaliyah's death and seeing him talk openly helped. It was clear to me then, that much of his bravado was a façade to cover a warm and loving soul. He was still sex-crazed, but I was hardly qualified to hold that against him.

Nick was next in line for the questioning. I started, 'Given the freedom to do anything to me, what would you do?'

Before he could answer, Curtis cut in 'Hells yeh, now the questions get interesting.'

Nick grinned at me. 'I was recently thinking that I'd love to try anal with you.'

I flushed. That was something I hadn't even tried with Jonah yet. 'Perhaps you should try it sometime then. Just be gentle… at first.'

Nick kissed me and squeezed my leg. The questioning continued for a while, then Nick asked me, 'When we made love the first time, I got the sense that you had some sexual experience. I also noticed the absence of… other tell-tale signs. Please tell me honestly — were you a virgin until then?'

His question sent a wave of panic through my nerves as my face paled. I knew that if I lied, he would doubt my integrity, but if I was honest, further questioning might arise. I had not had enough time to choose between them and I didn't want Nick to know that I had been with Jonah during the time that he was my teacher. 'No, you were not my first.'

Denise was so surprised at this that she lost her mouthful of drink. 'Oh my God Phoebe—you never told me of anyone before Nick. Come on girl—who was he? Fess up!'

And just like that my fears were justified. 'I'm sorry Denise. I cannot tell anyone, not even you. I promised him I would keep it secret.'

Denise pouted melodramatically, but I sensed that my lack of disclosure hurt her. After she had spent some time thinking it over, she blurted, '*Oh. My. God*! It was Mr. Collins, wasn't it? I've seen how well the two of you get along. I remember you telling me you had a crush on him—it was the last day of term one. He must've heard you, because he called you into his room immediately after! I recall thinking you had a shot, but you didn't mention it, so I assumed nothing happened.'

I blushed silently.

Nic's eyes widened. 'Is this true Phoebe? Did he…?'

Argh! I had to tread very carefully. 'Y…es, but it's not what you think, Nick. School had finished for the term, and we thought he was moving to your school. When the transfer fell through, he called it off.' At least this wasn't a complete lie.

Nick went on, 'Oh, WOW! This is just too weird. I thought there was something strange between the two of you, especially when I found you alone together at your birthday, but… Shit! Phoebe—he is old enough to be your father!'

'Why should that matter? It was legal, and I was still single at the time, so we weren't hurting anybody.'

Curtis had remained silent. I think I had managed to shock him too, which was quite a feat considering his own history. 'Wait, you said he called it off when the transfer went through. Does that mean you guys did it more than once?'

For Pete's sake, why couldn't they just drop it! 'Yes, we met several times during the holidays following term one, but he ended it before term two started. We decided to keep it a secret to save complicating things at school.'

A cloud of unease settled between me and Nick following this revelation.

Denise broke the ice, 'Well I don't see anything wrong with it. As Phoebe said, it was all legit. I say we move on and drink up!'

'Cheers to that!' Curtis agreed.

So, the drinking and the game continued, allowing Nick to loosen up a bit more. I snuggled in close to him as soon as I sensed his muscles relaxing, and he put his arms around me. I felt relieved to have dodged that bullet.

After several more rounds of drinks, Denise was being quizzed and Nick asked her, 'Have you ever kissed a girl?'

'No.'

Intrigued, Curtis followed up with, 'Have you ever wanted to kiss a girl?'

'Yes,' she responded with a giggle.

Curiosity got the better of me. 'Anyone in particular?'

She blushed and looked straight at me, and I suddenly got it. This provoked some strange thoughts and feelings for me. I had never thought of experimenting with Denise, or other girls, but at that moment the idea turned me on. I smiled, then looked to Nick, silently seeking permission.

He grinned. 'Go on then.'

So, I leaned in and kissed my best friend. The taste of vodka was incredibly strong on her breath, but she also tasted sweet, and her lips were much softer than any guys'. She was gentle with me at first, and I could hear the boys breathing heavily in the background, but then she increased the intensity, and it was like she was in my head, so I became lost in the moment. When we finished, I remained speechless for several minutes.

Later, Denise asked me, 'Ok, Phoebs. Have you fantasised about a threesome?'

I was incredibly drunk by this stage, so I giggled as I replied, 'Oh my, yes!'

Nick stared at me. 'Two guys with yourself, or a guy and girl?'

I giggled even more and looked directly at Nick.

'Both, but especially two men with myself.'

Nick gripped my leg. 'You amaze me Phoebe. I had no idea you were so… adventurous.'

Curtis capped off this round. 'Would you be willing to try a foursome, with us here tonight?'

'Yes, I would — if Nick and Denise are willing.'

Nick gaped at first, but, like with the rest of us, hormones took over, so it happened. The four of us became closer than ever that night.

It was a relief to wake up the next morning and not feel strange around Nick and my friends. Everyone seemed relaxed and no one was avoiding eye contact. It was like the activities of the night before were exactly what we needed to release tensions between us and form a stronger bond.

Nick even broached the topic of Jonah. 'I'm sorry if I seemed harsh or judgemental with you last night when you confessed about Jonah. I guess I was a little hurt that you'd kept it from me, but I had no right to be so severe.'

'It's okay. I'm glad you know now. I'm sorry I hid it from you for so long.'

Chapter Twenty-Eight

Diary extract dated Monday 7th January 2002

I did it! I got accepted into my first preference at university! I also ranked amongst the top 3% of graduating students in the state.

The Christmas holiday period came and went in the blink of an eye. I had a lot of fun and laughs with my family and friends over those two weeks. After New Year's, I spent the remainder of that time at my dad's house. Nick went along with me too, which was Dad's idea. He wanted to meet Nick, having heard so much about him. They got along splendidly, as expected. Sharing a love of Australian movies kept them talking and Dad even introduced Nick to a few, like *Dead Calm* and *Two Hands*.

Then the moment of truth finally arrived. When I saw the emails with my results and university offer, I squealed. I was at Jonah's place at the time, and I knew the first-round offers would come that day, so

I asked to borrow his computer. He was a little startled by the noise I made, then also by my sudden rush into his arms.

He chuckled. 'I assume you did well then, Phoebe?'

'First preference and top three percent!' I boasted.

He smiled and kissed me. 'Congratulations. Of course, I knew you would do it. What course did they offer?'

'The Advanced Bachelor of Arts.'

'Well, this is cause for celebration. Have a seat and I will get us a drink.'

I sat on the couch, and he opened a bottle of bubbly that had been chilling in the fridge. I guessed he saw this coming and had prepared accordingly. He returned with two full glasses, sat beside me, and handed me one. 'I toast to you Phoebe. This is to your past and future successes — cheers!'

'Thank you, Jonah. Cheers.' I sipped the wine, enjoying the sweet and fruity flavour as it went down easily.

'Assuming you accept the university's offer, which major do you think you will choose?' he asked.

'I haven't decided for sure yet, but most likely creative writing.'

He smiled. 'I look forward to reading your work.'

My phone rang then, and I glimpsed Nick's name. 'I'd better take this, sorry.'

'That is okay. You may use the study.'

I did so, then answered the call once the door had closed. 'Hi Nick.'

'Hi Phoebe. Where are you? I have some news to share with you.'

I figured he must have his offer too. 'I'm in the city. What is the news?'

'Can you come over to my place? I want to tell you in person.'

'Okay, I will get there as soon as I can.' We hung up, and I returned to the living room. 'I'm sorry Jonah, I have to go.'

He looked worried. 'Is everything okay?'

'Yes, I think so. Nick has something he wants to tell me in person. I also have my own news to tell him. Can I come back later tonight?'

'Yes, of course. I will be home.' We kissed goodbye, then I let myself out.

ℴℴ

On the train journey to Nick's house, I thought a lot about both of my lovers and about my future studies. I had been waiting for Nick's offer to arrive because it was hard to decide on a course of action without knowing where Nick was going to be. If he stayed in the state, it was possible that I could continue seeing them both, but then I would have to find a way of telling Nick about my need to see Jonah. If he went to Sydney, the choice would be harder.

Nick greeted me with a big smile, then kissed me deeply.

'Okay, Nick, the suspense is killing me. What is your news?'

'Okay, okay. They loved me, Phoebe! NIDA accepted me!' he beamed.

'Oh wow! That's awesome news!' I hugged him tight. That was it then. Big decision time.

'Will you come to Sydney with me, my dear?'

'I would like to Nick, I really would, but I need to sort out a few things before I can make a definite choice. It would mean a huge change for me.'

We sat down on his couch. 'I understand, Phoebe. Have you received your offer?'

I smiled then, feeling proud to tell him, 'Yes actually. I got my first pick and I scored within the top three percent of the state.'

'Wow! That is fantastic. If you choose to study in Sydney, you won't have trouble getting into a uni there.'

'That's one thing I'd need to be certain of. I think I'll have to defer my offer rather than reject it just in case I can't get something over there.'

He looked at me with a puzzled expression for a moment. 'Only one of the things? What else do you need to be sure of?'

I sighed. 'Well firstly, there is the fact that I'll be leaving my family and friends, so I need to be ready to deal with that. Then there's also the matter of living arrangements. Where would we live, how will we pay for rent and other expenses?'

He smiled again. 'That's something we don't have to worry about. My dad owns some property over there that we could live in rent-free. If we study full-time, we could both get a study allowance from the government to help us pay for our food and bills.'

'Wow! You've really thought this through already. That's a relief. But I still need to think about it. Can you give me a little time to work it out?'

'Yes, of course. I need to head over to Sydney next week to sort out my enrolment. I also plan to check out the flats that Dad has available now and choose which one I want. That should give you some time to think things through. I will come for your answer when I return.'

That gave me a little under two weeks. I hoped it was enough time to make up my mind.

'In the meantime, let's make the most of the time we have together this week,' he insisted.

We spent the rest of the week largely outdoors. He meant it when he said he wanted to make the most of our time together. We went to the beach one day, played mini golf with Denise and Curtis the next, then hiking, rock-climbing, and horse-riding. I also stayed over at Nick's house every night. I told Jonah that Nick was going away soon, so he understood my need to spend this time with him.

I did manage to fit in one visit to Jonah, though. It

was on the Wednesday following mini golf. I told Nick that I needed to attend to some personal business before retiring at his place in the evening.

Jonah grabbed me the moment I stepped through the door and whisked me away to the bedroom.

Once the passion subsided, I brought up the vexing issue, 'Nick is moving to Sydney to study this year.' He looked at me expectantly. 'I am thinking of going with him.'

His mood shifted instantly, and a frown darkened his expression. He must have been quietly confident that I would choose him, or at least choose to continue our current arrangement. 'I see.'

'I haven't decided if I'll go yet. I just wanted to tell you that I am considering it. Nick is going over there next week to sort out his enrolment and living arrangements. He wants my answer when he gets back.'

Jonah sighed and looked at me glumly. 'Hmm. Are you at least close to a decision?'

'I will confess that I am currently in favour of moving with him. Things seem much more real with Nick. I guess this is largely because I have been able to date him openly.'

Jonah began to reply, then he stopped himself.

I continued, 'My time with you, Jonah, has often felt like a fantasy. A really hot, steamy fantasy. I just can't imagine it any other way.'

At least he was able to smile a little at this. We both

fell quiet for a few minutes, then a look of realisation dawned on Jonah's face. 'You said Nick will be away in Sydney next week?'

'Yes. Why?'

'I want to take you on a short holiday, Phoebe. I would like a chance to spend some time out in the open with you. I do not know if this will impact on your decision, but either way it would be good for us. Do you remember my son, Heath?'

How could I forget? I wondered what sort of a holiday he had in mind. 'Yes, of course I remember Heath.'

'He will be coming to stay with me next week. It would be good for the three of us to go for a trip along the coast. I have a holiday house we can stay in.'

That did sound good, and it wasn't like I had much else planned. 'Okay, that would be nice.'

'Excellent. I will make some arrangements. Thank you, Phoebe.'

Chapter Twenty-Nine

Diary extract dated Tuesday 15th January 2002

For the first time, I began to scream ecstatically and loudly, without any restraint. It was impossible to hold back.

The day before our getaway, I rang Jonah to confirm the details. He told me little of his plans, but I was intrigued when he asked me if I had any issues with boats or sea sickness. I confessed that I'd had minimal exposure to sailing, but I was not averse to the idea.

The doorbell rang at the pre-arranged time. 'Hi Jonah.' We kissed briefly.

'Here let me take your bags. I do hope you followed my recommendations when packing.'

'Yes. I have swimwear, warm and cool weather clothes, and only one book. I have kept it minimal, so this is all I have.' I gestured toward the two small bags and my purse.

'I am pleased to hear it. Come on. Heath is waiting

in the car.' He had parked directly outside this time, rather than down the street in our usual spot.

When I got to the car, Heath stepped out of the front seat, offering it to me. 'Hello Phoebe. It's good to see you again.' His tone was very charming, but I detected a glint of something more indecent in his eyes.

'Hi Heath. Thank you.'

Jonah started driving and Heath continued talking, 'How've you been, Phoebe?'

'I've been well, thank you. And you, Heath?'

It felt a little awkward trying to carry on a conversation with someone I barely knew when he was sitting behind me.

'I've been great. I'm glad high school has finished. Now I have uni life to look forward to.'

'Oh, so did you just receive your offer too? How'd you go?' I asked.

'I aced it all. Advanced Bachelor of Arts for me.'

'Oh, wow! That's the same course I've been offered. Congratulations, Heath. What major?'

'Cheers. I plan to study media. I'd like to work in television or at least some form of journalism. So, did you just finish school this year too? I thought you'd have been at uni already.'

Since I knew so little about Heath, I figured Jonah didn't tell him much about me either. 'Yes, I just graduated. I'd like to study literature and creative writing.'

'Ah, so you're a bit of bookworm. There's something you have in common with Dad. I guess I'll see you around on campus.'

'Yes, maybe.'

We arrived at a marina, where Jonah parked and secured the car. He turned to me. 'Okay we are here. Now our vessel awaits.' He took our bags from the car and led me towards his sailing boat docked close by. The name *Hedone* made me smile, thanks to my studies in classical mythology. Heath told me it was a Northshore 27 cruiser — details that meant little to me.

Jonah busied himself with our bags when we embarked, so Heath helped me aboard. He looked at me fervidly when he gripped my hands to steady my feet. That, combined with the physical contact, sent signals rushing through my body, the sort that bypassed my brain entirely and made me blush.

We all went straight below deck, where a beautifully furnished interior took my breath away. It boasted a reasonable amount of space as well as two sleeping cabins. After packing our bags away, Jonah helped me into a lifejacket and handed me some pills. 'These are for motion sickness; in case you need them. We are going to cruise along the coast for the next two days, then we will spend two nights at my holiday house before we return.'

'I must say that this is all quite a surprise. I had no idea you had a boat. I didn't even know about the holiday house until recently. Do you have any other property hidden away somewhere?'

He grinned, giving me that cheeky smile of his that I had become so fond of. 'I like to maintain some mystery. It means that I can surprise you when the opportunity arises. Now, we must away!'

I watched both Jonah and Heath with fascination as they worked together hoisting the sails, starting the motor, and steering the yacht out of the harbour. It was all a very new experience for me. Once we were out in clear waters, Heath left Jonah at the tiller and summoned me below deck. 'I'm going to fix us all some refreshments. Would you mind giving me a hand, Phoebe?'

I followed him downstairs, where he took some cocktail ingredients from the fridge.

Sitting at the table to mix the drinks, he asked, 'So, what school did you go to Phoebe?'

I paused a moment to consider my answer carefully, but then I figured there was no harm in telling him the truth since his mum already knew. 'St. Teresa's.'

His smile widened as the facts occurred to him. 'Wait a minute! Isn't that Dad's work? Oh my God! He was your teacher!'

'Uh, yes. I figured you knew since your mum worked it out.'

He chuckled. 'That dirty bastard! Oh, sorry—no offence. I didn't mean for that to sound nasty or anything.'

'That's okay. No offence taken.'

'To be honest, I'm kinda proud of the ol' man for having the gall. How long have the two of you been seeing each other?' He poured the concoction he just made into three glasses and handed me one.

'About nine months now. It started at the end of term one when he was about to transfer to another school, but those plans fell through, so we had to keep it secret while I remained his pupil. Your mum caught us though. She had photos that she tried to blackmail Jonah with.' *Oh shit! I didn't mean to just blurt that out to him.* Somehow, he just made me feel so at ease that I completely let my guard down.

'Seriously? What a bitch! Oh, sorry—there I go again with my mouth. But then I did mean for that to sound a bit nasty. I'll admit that I have a low opinion of my mum. She hasn't been the best of parents. I wanted to stay with Dad when they split, but she refused to consider my preference and made it very hard for me to see him. She was an awful wife for Dad. They were always fighting for as long as I can remember.'

'Oh, geez, I'm sorry Heath. My own parents split when I was three, but I don't recall much fighting. They were pretty civil for the most part, so I can't begin to imagine what it would have been like for you.'

He motioned for me to head back upstairs. 'Ah,

it's okay. I got used to it and learnt some good coping mechanisms.' He gestured toward the drinks.

We took our cocktails back up into the fresh air. Jonah smiled when I returned then put one arm around me when I came up alongside him. He grabbed his glass from Heath with the other hand. 'Thank you, Heath. How are you feeling Phoebe? Any signs of sea sickness?'

'I'm fine. No symptoms of the sort.'

It felt good to be out at sea, with the fresh, salty breeze teasing the tendrils of my hair. I sat back and relaxed for the most part, while Jonah and Heath took turns steering. That night Jonah anchored the boat so that we could all lounge about in the saloon. We had a great time chatting the night away, first over dinner, then over a few rounds of cards. This was the first time that I caught a glimpse of Jonah's more social and familial side. He was in his element here and it was good to see. Exhausted by the time we settled into our beds, we spent our first night sleeping together without any sex.

Fishing was first on the agenda the next day and both men insisted that I have a go. Heath teased me a little by saying, 'The Collins family fishing rule is that you have to catch your own dinner otherwise you scale all the fish yourself.'

I looked to Jonah for sympathy, but he just grinned, which made me anxious, so I fumbled a lot with my rod. Seeing the trouble I was having, Jonah put his arms around me to aid my grip and casting. He also whispered in my ear, 'As always, I am willing to break the rules for you, Phoebe. I will take care of the scaling. Just enjoy yourself.'

This did a lot to ease my tension and I even managed to catch one fish big enough to keep. The others hauled in a decent amount between them, so we had ample for two meals.

ഔ

We reached our destination by mid-afternoon that day and when we arrived at Jonah's beach house, I gaped at the familiar place.

Seeing the look on my face, Jonah asked, 'What is it Phoebe? Is something wrong?'

'Oh, sorry. No, nothing is wrong. It is just that I have been here before. This is the house I stayed in over schoolies.'

This brought a grin to his face. 'Really? Now I am even more curious to know what you got up to that week. It is a pity I was unaware beforehand, else I would have waived the rental for you.'

We took our bags into the master bedroom where Jonah asked, 'Who stayed in this room?'

I blushed. 'Nick and I stayed in here. Denise and Curtis were in the room that Heath went into.'

He grabbed me and pulled me onto the bed. 'Now it is my turn to have you in this bed.' The heat of the moment took us then.

Afterwards, he left me resting while he headed out to the shops to get some food supplies for our meals.

I awoke to a knock at the bedroom door. 'Yes?'

'It's Heath. I brought you some water.'

I sat up and quickly threw my skimpy nightgown on before he walked in. He handed me a glass of ice-cold water then sat down on the side of the bed and grinned at me. 'I figured you would be feeling the effects of the heat. I know I am.'

'Um, thank you, Heath. That's very kind of you.'

He didn't bother to hide the fact that he was taking in the view. 'So, you stayed here for schoolies, huh?'

'Yes, I did. I had no idea your dad owned the place though.'

'I'm surprised I didn't see you that week. I was staying in Mum's shack just down the road.'

Gosh, I wondered just how much property the Collins family owned between them. 'It was a pretty crowded town that week and we mostly kept to ourselves during the day, so I guess that's why.'

'Who did you stay with?'

'Just my boyfriend Nick, best friend Denise, and her boyfriend, Curtis.'

A quizzical look came across his face then. 'Boyfriend?'

Oh right, I hadn't told him about Nick at all yet. 'Yes, I also have a boyfriend. Your dad knows all about it, although Nick doesn't know that I have been seeing your dad all this time.'

His grin of approval returned. 'Well, aren't you a saucy minx then?'

It felt as though my face turned the colour of a lobster. I didn't know how else to respond to that.

He placed a hand on one of my bare knees and added, 'The more I get to know you, Phoebe, the more I like you.' He started moving his hand up my thigh, all the while keeping his eyes fixed on mine. Their depths hypnotised me, and I felt powerless to stop him. The sound of the front door slamming shut broke the spell, however. He stood up. 'I'd better go and help Dad with dinner. See you again soon.'

My God! What was it about Heath? I knew then that spending time alone with him wouldn't be safe, but he enthralled me, and I couldn't stay away.

I got dressed, then headed downstairs to help. Jonah had bought some hot chips and pre-made salads, so all they needed to do was cook the fish they had scaled earlier that day. I put the oven on and popped the chips inside to keep them warm, then sat down while they took care of rest of the meal. They both occasionally looked at me, smiling as they cooked.

℘⊂ℛ

Things seriously heated up in the bedroom that night. While I am not usually one for graphically describing the details of my carnal activities, I feel it is necessary to give the following account of what happened between us this time because of the impact it had on my sexuality.

I was feeling refreshed from my afternoon nap, and Jonah, well I'm not sure where his energy came from, but he was insatiable. He did something a little unexpected while we were having sex that night. In the throes of passion, I suddenly felt a finger enter my backside.

'Does this feel okay, Phoebe?'

This was still unexplored territory for me. Nick hadn't made any attempts with me yet, despite his confession at schoolies. 'It is strange, but also good,' I said.

'I would like to gradually increase the number of fingers. Please stop me if it gets too painful at any point.'

'Okay.' The intensity of my pleasure grew with each digit, and I could feel myself slipping into an altered state of consciousness.

After the fourth one had been there a while, he asked, 'Would you like me to try the next step?'

Guessing at his meaning, I groaned pleasurably. 'Yes please.'

My assumption was not wrong. He switched body parts and my climax reached unimaginable heights.

Up until this point I had exercised a degree of control when expressing rapture, but what Jonah did to me that night unleashed something wild within me.

We showered together afterwards, kissing tenderly under the warm water. This was when he said it. 'God, I love you, Phoebe. Please do not go to Sydney. Stay with me. Be mine.'

I was not in any frame of mind for decision-making then, so I didn't say anything. I just kissed him more.

ဆာလ

Jonah collapsed in bed, but I couldn't sleep. The combination of an afternoon nap and that mad rush of hormones left me hyped, so I went downstairs to make some tea. I found Heath lounging in the living area with the television on quietly. When he saw me, he grinned and asked, 'So now you can't sleep either?'

I started brewing some chamomile tea. 'That's right. It must have been the afternoon nap.' I took my tea to the couch and sat next to him.

'Perhaps. For me it was probably all that noise.'

Oh crap! He'd heard me! 'Oops! Sorry Heath!' I blushed.

'Nah, it's okay. I really didn't mind. I'm glad you enjoyed yourself.'

He took a sip from a hip flask. 'Would you like a drink?'

I took the flask and sniffed the potent smelling

contents. 'What is it?'

'Malt whisky—the good stuff.'

I sipped it. 'Wow—that's strong!'

He smiled. 'You haven't tried straight whisky before, have you?'

'No, not really. I don't drink spirits straight.'

He took another swig, then handed it back to me. I accepted it. This time I knew what I was in for, so I could appreciate the flavour more.

'There isn't much on TV. Do you mind if I put some music on?' he asked.

'Go for it.'

He got up and put some CDs in the stereo, then set it to shuffle play. The funky sounds of Jamiroquai greeted me.

'Not a bad choice,' I commented.

'Oh, so you like Jay Kay?'

'Yes, I do. I'm more of Euro-trance fan, but I like funk and R&B as well. All good stuff to dance to.'

He returned to the couch, only I noticed he sat somewhat closer to me. 'Oh, so you dance too? I'd like to see that.'

'Perhaps you will one day, especially since we're going to the same campus.' We both drank more whisky. I could feel it going to my head. 'Tell me about yourself, Heath.'

He grinned. 'Me? What would you like to know?'

'I don't know, tell me anything.' Another sip, then I noticed my forgotten cup of tea. *Oh well!*

'Okay, but for everything I reveal, you'll have to give me something related about yourself.'

'Okay, it's a deal.'

He paused to think a moment. 'Let's start simple. I like action movies.'

'Alright, I don't mind them myself, but I really like romantic movies,' I confessed.

'*Romance* huh?' he winked at me, 'I like to play basketball.'

I had been wondering if he played any sport. 'Nice. I play netball.'

He gave me sly smile. 'Do you play competitively?'

'I did at school. I was in the A–Grade team with your dad as my coach.'

He laughed at that. 'He saw you in a netball skirt regularly. No wonder he couldn't keep away from you.'

I giggled.

'I drive a red BMW,' he continued.

'Mm, a fancy car. I don't drive.'

His eyes narrowed. 'Oh? Why not?'

I shrugged. 'I just never got around to learning. Everyone else I knew was happy to drive me around, so I didn't bother.'

'But driving is so fun and liberating. I would love to teach you.'

I never really thought of it like that. Driving had always seemed so utilitarian. I smiled. 'Okay, maybe we could give that a go sometime. Now tell me some more… personal stuff.' I chortled.

His eyes gleamed then and we both drank some more whisky. 'Hm, well you asked for this. The first time I had sex was when I was thirteen and it was with a sixteen-year-old girl in the back of her car.'

Wow! So young! 'Indeed. Well, your dad took my virginity when I was eighteen and we were in his classroom.'

'You are full of surprises, Phoebe. I assumed you started earlier given how… sensual you are now.'

I feigned a coy smile. Then, he continued, 'I've slept with sixteen different girls and eight boys.'

I almost choked then. 'Holy… geez that's a lot! How many of them did you actually date?'

'Only four of them were girlfriends.' Heath was younger than me, yet he had a lot more experience than I could fathom.

'I have been with three different guys and one girl.'

His left brow rose. 'Okay so I can guess who two of those are based on what I have learned from you. The other two?'

I laughed. 'You'll have to share the right sort of info to get that out of me.'

'Oh, so that's how you want to play this. Alright, let me think now… Ah, yes of course. The most other people I've had sex with at one time is two.'

I skulled the last of the flask and investigated it

sullenly.

He stood up, swaying a little. 'Fear not. I have a stash.' He stumbled a bit as he walked over to the kitchen.

Giggling, I imagined him trying and failing to walk a straight-line at the request of a police officer.

He returned with a bottle of vodka and two glasses. When he sat down, even closer to me, he poured us each a drink. Our legs were touching, the sensation very distracting.

'Three,' I replied simply.

'Three what?'

I just smiled at him.

He thought a moment, then remembered what we were talking about. 'Oh right. So those other two people were at the same time as either your boyfriend, or my dad, right?'

'Right.'

He swallowed a large amount of his drink. Then went on, 'Okay, time to up the stakes. I'm gonna tell you something that few people know about. In fact, I haven't told anyone about some of the details I'm about to reveal. I'm only doing this because I strongly feel that I can trust you, Phoebe.'

I paused for a strong intake of breath. 'Go on. Your secrets are safe with me.'

'I'm a voyeur.' I just looked at him, blinking. He continued. 'I enjoy watching it almost as much as doing it, sometimes more. It started when I was young, probably around eleven. I used to sneak up to my parents' room and spy on them through the bedroom door. I learned a lot about sex this way. I've watched a lot of porn videos too, but they aren't as good as the real thing.'

This was something I knew little of, but intrigued me all the same. 'Oh wow. Is it the spying aspect that you enjoy?'

'Not always. Part of the reason I have bedded so many people is because I have often asked to openly watch couples I knew. This would occasionally end in threesomes. But the spying is also very thrilling in its own right because of the adrenaline rush I get from the fear of getting caught. When I first heard you with Dad earlier, I couldn't help myself. Sorry.'

This last bit of his confession caught me off guard and I began choking on the vodka.

He began to pat my back. 'Are you okay? Can I get you some water?' I nodded. He jumped up and fetched me the drink. When he sat back down, he assumed the same position and continued patting my back. 'Sorry if that came as a bit of a shock.'

I sipped the water and regained my composure. 'It's okay. I was just a little startled, that's all. To be honest, I don't mind if you watch me. The idea kind of... excites me.'

He grinned widely. Then his hand dropped to my bare leg and his gaze transfixed me. 'Now it's your turn. What's your deepest, darkest secret, Phoebe?'

What was left for me to tell him? 'I don't know what else to say, Heath. You already know about my affair with your dad. That's been my big secret of late.' He looked at me expectantly. I thought for a few minutes, then something occurred to me that I was only just coming to realise about myself. 'If I'm honest with myself, I think I would have to say that I can't be happy with just one sexual partner. I need variety. I think that's why I have found it so hard to choose between Nick and Jonah.'

'Why do you have to choose?' he asked.

'Because Nick is moving to Sydney and wants me to go with him. And because your dad asked me to make the choice.'

His hand had moved as high as it could get while still resting on my leg, lifting the hem of my summer dress to maintain contact with my skin. It began to creep further inwards. 'If it makes any difference to your decision, I would be sad to see you leave.'

With that he leaned in and kissed me. His lips felt soft but packed a lot of force behind them. He didn't shy away from using his tongue either. He tasted of alcohol and his cologne smelt strong. While I didn't recognise it, I could detect hints of sandalwood in the fragrance. He was very much in tune with me, reminding me of that time with Denise; yet he was more aggressive about it, like his father.

I climbed on top of him, and his lips travelled to my neck. I was hardly even conscious of removing his pants. Before I knew it, he was inside me and I gave into my urges.

I eventually retired to my bed, but the hang-over that followed made for a rather unpleasant morning. Jonah didn't know about my late-night binge with Heath, so he was quite concerned and spent the morning nursing me. I was growing fond of this side of him and when I thought back over the years, I remembered numerous occasions where he was attentive like this. It got me thinking that I could get used to this side of Jonah.

I came good in the afternoon, much to everyone's relief, so we took a trip to the beach. When Jonah wasn't looking, Heath took a moment to stand directly next to me, grab my backside and whisper his approval of my swimsuit.

I spent a little time in the water, but for the most part, I enjoyed the opportunity to lounge on the sand and read, while the guys played various ball sports. This book was *The Monk* by Matthew Lewis, an interesting blend of Gothic and Libertine, my two favourite genres.

After a while, I dozed off in the sun, the book over my face. I woke up to Jonah kissing me gently. He smiled when I opened my eyes.

'Welcome back, Phoebe.'

'Mm, hi, Jonah.' Remembering my book, I surveyed the sand.

'Looking for this?' Jonah handed it to me.

'Ah, yes. Thank you.'

'A curious read, this one. Let me know what you think of it when you finish.'

'Certainly.'

He stood and offered a hand to help me up, then gripped me tight as we walked back to the house.

Chapter Thirty

Diary extract dated Friday 18th January 2002

All I could think to do was ring Jonah. I grabbed my mobile from my pocket.

'Hello Phoebe.' His voice coming across the phone line was so soothing. 'Are you crying Phoebe? What is wrong?'

I could almost feel his embrace.

'Phoebe? What is it? Where are you?'

I hardly knew anymore. 'I feel... so cold.'

'Phoebe?'

I dropped the phone and darkness overcame me.

The rest of the holiday continued much like it had started, only with Jonah being more attentive and affectionate, while Heath continued his filtrating, which I responded to in kind when alone.

Jonah took me home mid-afternoon that Friday. He helped with the bags, then kissed me goodbye at my door. It felt intense, and I remember thinking at the time it was nice not hiding so much.

I didn't notice him until Jonah had driven off, when he stepped out of the car and walked up to me with the most crestfallen look on his face. *No! I didn't want Nick to find out like this!* I began to tear up.

He ascended my front steps, stopping one down from me. 'I guess you have made your decision then.'

They trickled down my face. 'Oh God, Nick! I am so sorry! I—'

'You what? Couldn't wait to break my heart before jumping back in bed with your teacher?' Nick's tone shifted to one of pure rage.

I stood there in stunned silence. I just didn't know what to say. I didn't have a leg to stand on this time.

'How soon after I left did you do it?'

'I... We...' Words failed me as I stuttered senselessly.

'*How soon Phoebe*? Was it two days? One, or less?'

I just looked at him pitifully as I wept remorsefully.

'It was less, wasn't it?'

I remained motionless.

'*Wasn't it?*'

I looked down. I couldn't face him anymore.

'*Oh fuck!* You never really stopped seeing him, did you? All those times we just bumped into him. The long hours you spent at school. Then your birthday. It all makes sense now. *Shit!*'

I moved to embrace him. I wanted him to feel how sorry I was, but he just stepped back, letting me collapse to the ground in a fit of sobbing.

'*Don't touch me—you whore!*'

Then he ran off to his car and drove away, leaving me in a mess at the bottom of the steps. I felt so bad for Nick that I didn't even notice I was bleeding. That was when I rang Jonah, just before blacking out....

The next thing I remembered; the bright lights of my hospital room filled my vision. I stirred a little then the pain in my head, my neck, and my abdomen overwhelmed me, and I groaned loudly.

'Phoebe? You are awake at last!'

I turned and saw Jonah looking at me. He gripped my hand. 'What...? Where... am I?' I asked groggily.

'Oh God, Phoebe. You had me so worried.'

'And me too,' said another voice. I turned a little further and saw Heath.

Jonah continued, 'You are in hospital now, but you had a fall on the front steps of your home.'

The memory of Nick came flooding back to me

and I winced.

Mistaking my expression for physical pain, which wasn't far from the truth, Jonah buzzed for a nurse to come and tend to me. She fussed about me for a bit, checking my vitals.

'Hello Phoebe. My name is Judy. How are you feeling?'

'Sore. My neck feels stiff too.'

'Yes, I imagine it does. It seems that you had a nasty fall. Do you remember what happened?'

I did, well mostly, but I wasn't in the mood to give specifics. 'I think so, but the details are still a little fuzzy. I tripped on the steps.'

'I can give you a little more pain relief, but we have to be careful not to overdo it okay?'

'Okay.'

She pumped something into my drip. 'You are going to be okay, but we will need to keep you in here for a few days. I am going leave you in the loving hands of these gentlemen for a bit now, but I will be back soon.'

I looked back at Jonah, who grabbed my hand again. 'There is something else. When you rang me, Phoebe, I could not make much sense of the call, but I had not driven far from your house. I made a guess and returned there, which was where I found you. You were at the bottom of your steps... in a pool of blood.' He paused for a bit before continuing, 'I could not tell where it was coming from at first, but...

we have since learnt that you miscarried.'

I gaped at him in with wide eyes.

Jonah clarified, 'You were approximately six weeks pregnant, Phoebe.'

Pregnant? How could I have been? I had been so careful with the pill. I counted back and realised that I had in fact missed my last period, although I overlooked it amidst all the excitement of the last two weeks. I did some more mental sums and worked out that I would have conceived around the start of December. It could have been either Jonah's or Nick's. I figured it was probably just as well since I had been drinking a lot since then, so the baby probably wouldn't have been very healthy if it came to term. It was also the worst timing, but if this was a blessing, the horrendous cramps I suffered disguised it well. 'I had no idea, Jonah. I swear.'

'It is okay, Phoebe. I know you would not have kept something like that from me if you knew. By the way, I sent some brief text messages from your phone to your family and friends to let them know you are in hospital. I imagine some of them will arrive soon. Should I make myself scarce?'

It would be hard to explain why they were here, but I didn't care about that at the time. I needed Jonah. 'No, please stay. Just make up some excuse for being here.'

Almost as though he was psychic, I heard Mum's voice as she came rushing through my door. 'Oh, sweetheart. I came as soon as I heard.' She paused briefly, looking a little confused when she saw Jonah and Heath, then moved up to hug me. 'Are you okay? How are you feeling?'

'I'm very sore. The nurse said I will be okay, but I need to stay here for a few days.'

She caught a glimpse of the blood stains between my legs, alarming her further. 'Oh my, Phoebe— what happened?'

'I tripped down the front steps and passed out. Um… apparently, I miscarried.'

'Oh no sweetie, I am so sorry.' She teared up and hugged me again. Then she suddenly pulled back as something occurred to her. 'Where is Nick? Shouldn't he be here? And what are you doing here, Jonah and…?'

He introduced Heath, then explained, 'My son recently became good friends with Phoebe. We were in the area, and as we drove past your house, Heath noticed Phoebe collapsed at the bottom of the steps. He was the one who called the ambulance.'

She nodded. 'That's very lucky. Thank you, Heath. You may have saved my daughter's life. But what of Nick?'

I sighed miserably. 'We had a fight just before this….'

'Oh God—he didn't do this to you did he?' Mum asked.

I noticed Jonah and Heath stiffen to attention at

this news, both frowning.

When I thought about it, Nick kind of did do it unknowingly, but I didn't want him to take any blame for this. 'No. He left before it happened. He ran off and it was when I was running after him that I tripped.'

'Does he know you're in hospital?' she asked.

Jonah stepped up then. 'Yes, I messaged him. I had no idea about their fight though.'

'Well fight or no fight, if he loves my daughter he ought to be here. I am going to call him.'

'Please don't, Mum.' I was too late though, Mum had already grabbed my phone and stepped out of the room.

Once she left, Jonah piped up again, 'Was it because of me? Did he see us, Phoebe?'

There was no point hiding it from Jonah, so I nodded.

'Oh God, Phoebe, I am so sorry. I had no idea he was there. I guess that is why you were crying on the phone to me.'

My eyes began to moisten again as I remembered more of the incident. 'He said such nasty things to me,' I muttered.

'It is okay, Phoebe. You do not have to tell me all the details. Just try to get some rest.'

Mum returned looking very cross.

'Did you reach him?' I asked.

'Yes, I did. I am very disappointed in that young

man; I think I held him in higher esteem than he deserved. Suffice to say he will not be visiting you. I am sorry, Phoebe. I tried.'

I guessed he didn't tell her the full story. At least I could still give him some credit for that.

☙❧

I ended up staying for a full week. It took a while for the bleeding to subside, and I had a minor head injury they wanted to monitor too. During that time, I received regular visits from both of my parents, Denise, Jonah, and Heath.

Denise was the only one I told the full truth to in the end. While Jonah and Heath heard about the nature of my fight with Nick, I didn't want to tell them about how I reached out to Nick. Curtis has also told her Nick's side of the story, which was why Curtis didn't visit me right away. He was too angry to see me at first, but then Denise talked him around and they called in the day before my discharge. According to Curtis, Mum didn't tell Nick about the miscarriage, so Curtis had no idea until I told him.

'So, who was the father?' Curtis asked coldly.

'I don't know. It could have been either of them.'

He shook his head in disbelief. 'How could you do this to Nick—to all of us? You lied to the lot of us for all this time.'

'I'm sorry Curtis, really, I am. I needed them both, but I was too scared to open up to anyone about

Jonah. Given the way Nick reacted, I doubt he would have accepted it even if I told him from the start.'

'Maybe not, but you should have given him that choice.'

The guilt and pain I felt for Nick flooded back then and I began to cry. Denise sat on the side of the bed to comfort me. 'Curtis, please. Phoebe is still recovering from her injuries.'

'I'm sorry, Phoebe. I really am trying to understand where you are coming from.'

I wiped my eyes and blew my nose. 'It's okay, Denise. I need to work through this. Much of the pain I feel is because I did wrong by Nick. I see that now, but lust and other strong feelings consumed me, blinding me to reason. From now on, I'll adopt a full disclosure policy.'

Curtis sighed. 'Did you even love Nick?'

'Yes, I really did. I still do. That's why it hurts so much to see the pain I caused him.'

'I am content with that for now, thank you, Phoebe. I'm sorry for what happened to you, I really am.'

They left soon after that.

When I got home, I found a letter in my mailbox from Nick. There was no stamp on it, so I assumed he hand delivered it. I took it to my room to read, asking Mum to give me some time alone with it.

Dear Phoebe,

I am sorry to hear about the injuries you suffered following our altercation. My pain eased a little when I heard that you have recovered well. I also apologise for not visiting you, but please understand that seeing you would have been too much like rubbing salt on some very raw wounds.

Curtis told me about the miscarriage. Perhaps this was a blessing in disguise. Neither of us would have been ready to raise a child—that is if it was even mine, which brings me to my next point.

The fact that Jonah was your teacher at the time that you were seeing him is of no concern to me, so please rest assured that this potentially career-destroying secret is safe with me. I have no taste for vengeance.

What was a concern to me was the fact that you cheated on me. It is true that I would not have easily accepted your need for a second partner. In fact, given the choice now I cannot accept it, but it was unfair of you to decide this for me and then go behind my back and do it without my knowledge or consent. I offered you my heart completely and all I wanted in return was for you to do the same for me, but how could you do this when you divided your affections between two men?

I will be leaving for Sydney on the 8th February and it saddens me to know that I will not be taking you with me, but given all that has transpired, I feel that this is for the best. I cannot live with a woman whom I doubt, and I don't know if it would be possible to trust you again. So, this is it, this is goodbye. Please do not try to contact me.

From Nick.

By the time I finished reading it, my tears soaked much of the letter. I folded it and put it in my diary, then curled up on my bed and wept harder than ever before.

Chapter Thirty-One

Diary extract dated Monday 28th January 2002

Jonah asked for my decision today. While Nick was no longer an option for me, Jonah still wanted to know whether I would prefer a casual relationship, or something more.

I spent a few days following my return home thinking and crying. I wasn't in the mood to see or talk to anyone, not until the following Monday. This was when I asked Jonah to pick me up and take me to his place. I still felt weary following my ordeal, so I wasn't up for much exercise. I also insisted that Heath be there when I arrive.

I hugged them both when I got there, then sat on the couch. We started with a little small talk, then I handed Jonah the letter that Nick had written.

When he finished, he moved in close to hold me. 'I am sorry Phoebe.'

Heath asked, 'Is it okay if I read it?'

'Yes, please do.'

Then having done so, he sat on the other side of me to comfort me.

I took a deep breath, then spoke up. 'Heath, have you told your dad about what happened?'

He went pale. 'Um, no, but…'

'I have decided that I need to be more honest with all my partners, lovers, or whatever you want to call yourselves, from now on. So, here goes…' I took another deep breath. 'Jonah, Heath and I had sex when we were staying at your beach house.'

There was an awkward silence in the room for several minutes, during which time Jonah stood up and paced the room, while Heath sat hunched over with his head down.

When Jonah was eventually ready to talk, it took him several attempts. He sat back down next to me, and the words finally came, 'Thank you for your candour, Phoebe. I cannot fault either of you for what happened, especially since Phoebe and I have not made any commitments to each other. That said, I am not exactly pleased by the news. The idea of sharing a lover with my son makes me feel somewhat uncomfortable. I also have fatherly concerns for you, Heath, that I will not voice in this forum, but I will bring them up with you later. There is more that I would like to discuss with you Phoebe, but first I need some tea.'

He got up and busied himself in the kitchen.

Heath stood and started to make for his room, but Jonah stopped him. 'Sit down, Heath. You went and involved yourself in this, so now you must hear the rest of what I am to say.'

Heath promptly did as Jonah asked, all the while remaining silent.

Jonah returned with tea for us both, then retrieved his own and sat down. 'Now Phoebe, I know it is not quite the end of January, but circumstances have changed, so I would like to know what you have decided. Nick has clearly made part of the choice for you, but I would still like to know where I stand. Do you want to remain my casual lover, or do you want to become my exclusive partner?'

I thought about his question for a moment. 'I have very strong feelings for you Jonah, I always have. Which is why I could not be entirely content with something casual, but my ability to be your partner is going to be conditional. I am going to throw the choice back to you now because I need you to understand that a monogamous relationship won't satisfy me.'

He seemed surprised by this turn of events. 'But why, Phoebe? Do I not fulfil your needs?'

'It's because all the experiences I've had over the last nine months have shown me that I need variety. I have different desires that a single man cannot sate.'

He pondered my words while sipping his tea. 'Okay, I will try it your way, Phoebe. I cannot promise that I will always be happy about it, and I have other concerns, but I will attempt it. I have two provisos though. Firstly, you must take all precautions to protect your health and my own. Secondly, I want you to keep me in the loop, so please tell me about every encounter you have.'

This lifted my mood considerably. I threw my arms around him and kissed him on the cheek. 'Thank you, Jonah!'

'Now there is one other matter to discuss. Phoebe, as you know, Heath will be going to the same university as you. Because of this and other family issues, we have decided that he will reside here with me until he is ready to move out on his own. Firstly, do you have any issues with coming here to see me while Heath is here?'

I smiled. 'No, of course not.'

'And Heath, do you have any issues with Phoebe visiting me while you live here?'

Heath grinned as the weight of the room lifted. 'Well, no.'

Jonah relaxed and smiled. 'Good, I am glad that is settled then.'

Chapter Thirty-Two

Diary extract dated Thursday 7th February 2002

I have been a fool to think that I can find true happiness in the arms of a man who is more than twice my age.

For the most part, things sailed smoothly for several days following my discussion with Jonah and Heath. While I appreciated the freedom to choose other partners, time alone with Jonah satisfied me for a while. I still hadn't told Mum about him yet; I was trying to find a way of breaking the news to her.

Heath eased up on the flirting, although he could never really stop because that was the way he interacted with most people. We did, however, develop a good friendship.

There were still moments where grief overcame me when I thought about Nick. When this occurred in Jonah's presence, he was very understanding and comforting. Mum and Denise were also very supportive during this time. Of course, Denise commonly used retail therapy for such occasions, so she took me shopping at the Central Plaza on the day before Nick was due to leave.

The outing was fun up until we bumped into Curtis and Nick in the lifts. Denise squealed with delight at the sight of Curtis, and they greeted each other with a kiss, leaving Nick and me to stand there in painful silence. The lifts were notoriously slow, and this time it felt like we were never going to reach our floor. After the initial glimpse I turned away to avoid eye contact. Tears were trickling lightly down my face.

Thankfully, Denise kept her embrace short, so she was able to see my reaction. 'Oh God, I'm sorry Phoebe.' She took me into her arms, standing between Nick and me. 'Sorry, but we will have to catch up again soon, Curtis.'

He nodded. 'Yes, I understand.'

Before this journey—which was beginning to feel like a decent into hell—came to an end, I looked at Nick one last time. 'I really am sorry, Nick.'

With a large intake of breath, he turned to look at me; dark circles framing his eyes. He spoke with a dejected voice, 'I know. I'm sorry too. Goodbye, Phoebe.' Stepping out of the lift, he walked out of my life.

We all made our exit too, but Denise took me in a different direction. We found a seat and she gave me a chance to let it out.

After the shopping, I asked Denise to drop me off at Jonah's place. I knew she was busy that night and I felt a need to see him. The shock came the moment I opened his apartment door. I could hardly believe my eyes. None other than Sandra, the blackmailing bitch, was standing behind Jonah, who sat at his dining table, and she was massaging his shoulders.

They both looked up at me when I entered. Jonah spoke first, 'I am sorry, Phoebe, but now is not a good time.'

Then Sandra grinned, although on her this looked more like the malevolent sneer of an evil queen from a Brothers Grimm story. 'That's right, the adults are busy talking, so run along now, *child*.'

Those words cut deep. Under any normal circumstances, I would have responded more impetuously to such venom, but seeing her with Jonah like that—and his own dismissal of me—left me no choice. I fled.

I ran back to the lift, and once inside, I sank to the floor and wept like a baby. When I reached the ground floor, I staggered out into the street, where I wandered aimlessly, unable to make sense of my surroundings through the droplets of salty water that kept flowing from my eyes. I eventually found a park bench to collapse on and rang my mother. 'M-Mum.' I sobbed.

'Oh God, sweetheart, what's wrong?'

'Please… pick me up.' My hands were trembling, and it took all my strength to hold the phone to my ear.

'Yes, of course. Where are you?'

I had no idea, so I looked around for a landmark. Startling, I recognised St. Teresa's across the road. 'Behind the school.'

'Okay hun, I will be right there.'

I curled up and waited for her. So, this was what it was like to have one's heart completely broken. The pain I suffered when Nick ended our relationship was tortuous, but Jonah's comforting arms had buffered that. Without his affections, the agony became unbearable. I felt so alone. It occurred to me that I was stupid to trust my heart to one man, especially someone so much older than me.

When I got into Mum's car, she asked, 'What happened? Why are you so upset?'

I wasn't ready to tell her the full truth yet. 'I bumped into Nick. It wasn't pleasant.'

'Oh, sweetie, I am sorry. Wow—he really has done a number on you.' She took me home and treated me to sushi that night, although I couldn't eat much.

After dinner, I went to my room and cried myself to sleep.

Chapter Thirty-Three

Diary extract back-dated Sunday 24ᵗʰ February 2002

Mental note: If I survive this, I swear to myself,
here and now, that I will never touch drugs again.

I spent the fortnight that followed in a strange
type of emotional disconnect. I had cried so
much since breaking up with Nick that the
incident with Jonah pulled out the last of my
reserves. My heart went numb.

Jonah made several attempts to call me and even
visit me during that time, but I ignored them all. I
figured that hearing his voice or seeing him would
just make things worse. Even Heath made a few
attempts to contact me. I didn't have his number in
my phone, so I didn't recognise it at first and I
ignored calls from unknown numbers as a rule. He
eventually sent me a text message: THIS IS HEATH.
ARE YOU OK, PHOEBE? YOU HAVE US VERY WORRIED.
PLEASE CALL ME.

I considered it, but fear that his dad might take

over the phone call stopped me. Instead of reaching out to friends, or confronting Jonah, I employed a rather stupid and reckless strategy to deal with the losses I felt. It seemed perfectly reasonable to me at the time, of course, but you know what they say about hindsight.

I got in touch with some of the girls from school with connections in certain circles, and hit the night club scene as often and as hard as I could. I tried a few different drugs, including speed, cocaine, and ecstasy. The latter became my favourite. I also hooked up with lots of random strangers, both men and women. I lost count of how many people I slept with during this dark, mind-altered phase.

On one such occasion, the girls took me to a private warehouse party. There were plenty of pills freely available to girls that night and I took full advantage of this fact. After hours of dancing and flirting with a group of well dressed, attractive guys, I found myself entering a private room where they stripped me naked and passed me around like a strumpet. I didn't feel great about the situation, but I was beyond caring, so I let it happen. One of them took quite a liking to me and became a regular dance partner at future parties and club nights. He introduced himself as Vince.

ഇരു

It was a Saturday night, which meant the best venues

were open. We started out at an R&B club to warm up. Denise was there too, but she called it a night at around eleven, leaving with Curtis. The rest of us moved on to *The Vault*, which was our favourite electronica spot. Denise hadn't seen me using any drugs, although she had noticed some changes in my behaviour which worried her.

When we entered the next venue, Vince caught sight of me and proceeded to greet me with a kiss. Then he bought me a drink and slipped me some E before dancing with me for a bit. 'Let's go somewhere more fun.'

'I like fun,' I giggled.

'Yes, I know,' he replied in a lewd tone.

We left the club, and he took me for a walk to a nearby hotel. I didn't catch the name of the place—I was too heavily intoxicated. He took us straight through the lobby. We spent the elevator ride pashing, and groping each other, then I giggled all the way down the hall.

As soon as we entered the room the hairs on the back of my neck stood up. Something looked very wrong here. There were ropes and chains all over the place and a series of what looked like torture devices alongside the bed.

'*Hell no!*' I cried.

Then I made for the door, but Vince grabbed me tight and stuffed a gag in my mouth. He pushed me down on the bed and fastened my ankles and wrists with ropes. Then he cut my clothes away and forced himself upon me. Afterwards, he spent some time hitting me with various implements, each more intense than the last. I kept trying to scream out, but the rubber ball in my mouth muffled the sound. He had his way with me several times and assaulted me during the intervals. When he had finished with the flogging tools, he moved onto the blades. He didn't make any deep or large wounds, just shallow grazes and lacerations that stung like hell. This was when I made the mental oath to myself.

After a while the pain got so overwhelming that I passed out.

…

When I came to, I found that I was alone in the makeshift dungeon. I was still tied to the bed, but the gag had been removed. I cried out, 'Vince?'

No answer.

'Is anyone there?'

Nothing but silence.

I struggled with the ropes for a while and eventually got my left arm and leg free. I reached around for something to help me with the rest of the ropes, but all the knives were on the other side of the bed, well out of my reach.

I rolled over so that I could feel around under the bed, where I managed to grip something with my foot. I pulled it out and found that it was my handbag. Hope returned. I dragged it up so that I could grab it with my free hand and emptied the contents onto my chest. *Shit!* My wallet and keys were gone. Thankfully, my phone remained.

I began dialling emergency services but stopped myself when I remembered the drugs in my system. I considered calling Mum or Denise, but they weren't strong enough to fight Vince and I didn't want to put them in danger. So, I scrolled through my contacts for options. It was a challenge doing this one-handed and with my non-dominant hand at that. I found Heath's number. Not knowing who else to call, I rang him. It was around three in the morning by this stage and he failed to answer the first time. He must have been sleeping. I kept trying and eventually he answered with a yawn followed by, 'Hello?'

My whole body was shaking, and this extended to my voice when I spoke. 'Heath?'

'My God, Phoebe, is that you?'

'Yes. Please help.' I sobbed. At that moment I could hear footsteps and hushed voices down the hall.

'Fuck! Are you okay? Where are you?' he asked.

I lowered my own voice. 'I don't know—some cheap looking hotel near *The Vault*. I think it's room four-something. I've been raped and left tied to the bed.'

'*Christ Phoebe*! Why haven't you called the police?'

The voices were approaching.

'Because I'm dosed up on pills.'

'Geez woman. Okay, I'm coming. Hang in there, okay?'

Before I could sign off, the door flung open and Vince entered with two of his mates. When he saw me holding my phone he rushed in and grabbed it, then struck me hard across the face. 'Who were you talking to, bitch? Was it the cops?'

'No cops, I swear,' I cried.

He looked at my phone. Then sniggered as he addressed his mates, 'Hey guys, there's some sad fuck called Heath on the line.' He spoke into the phone then. 'Sorry Heath, but the slut is unavailable now. See ya.' He flung the phone across the room and it smashed against the wall. 'That ought to stop ya future attempts, ya cunt.'

One of his mates approached me and inspected the ropes. 'Jesus, Vince—your rope work's pretty shit. You'd better let me handle it. I'll give you more lessons later.' He re-tied the knots around my left limbs, then fixed the ones on my right. He smirked at me, then said, 'You won't be getting out of these so easily, my dear.' The way he said those last two words made me feel sick. It was like a cruel mockery of what I had lost.

What followed was far too horrendous and traumatic for me to put into words. Suffice to say that the scars I left with were not only emotional.

When they were done, they dressed me in some old rags, then dumped me in a laneway beside the hotel. I was too sore to move, so I pulled myself up into the foetal position, and whimpered, too weak for anything else.

...

'Phoebe, is that you?' I heard a man's voice calling out to me down the alley, so I looked up. 'My *God! Phoebe?*' He approached. Then I heard him call out, '*Dad—I found her*!' The sound of running footsteps. 'Christ Phoebe, what has that bastard done to you?' He crouched down in front of me. I just blinked at him.

'Phoebe?' the other man inquired. He sounded scared. 'Oh no, Phoebe. What...' he wept.

I felt one of them scoop me up into his arms. He smelt familiar, like home. I finally felt safe, so I went to sleep.

ৡ০৫

I awoke in a bright, white room, with lots of beeping, buzzing, banging, and babbling sounds around me. It took me a while to get my bearings. Then I realise that I was in a hospital.

I turned my head to look around and found two men at my bedside. When they saw me waking up, they moved closer. I tried to speak, but my throat was too dry and sore, so I just made an odd noise.

The older of the two men, who looked like my English teacher, sat close beside me and helped me drink some water. 'Here, Phoebe. Don't try to talk yet. The doctor said your throat will be raw for a few days. Just take small sips.' He placed the cup back on the table. Then asked, 'How is your right hand? Do you think you could write with it?'

I flexed my fingers. While the wrist was quite sore, I seemed to have reasonable control of my digits. I gently nodded my head.

He gave me a pad of paper and a pen, then asked, 'How much can you remember?'

'Not much,' I wrote.

He frowned. 'Do you know who I am?'

'Are you Mr. Collins?'

Tears started to form in his eyes, and he shook his head. 'Yes, I am, but you haven't called me that for months now, Phoebe. Do you know who this is?' He pointed to the other man.

'No, sorry.'

This distressed them both. Mr. Collins used my buzzer to call a nurse, then introduced the other man as his son, Heath. When the nurse came, he told her, 'She has woken up, but she has some memory troubles.'

'Ok, thank you for letting me know. It's not unusual for someone who has suffered so much to develop amnesia. I will call for a doctor to come and conduct some more tests.'

The nurse approached me then. She smiled warmly. 'Hello Phoebe. I am Veronika. How is your throat?

I wrote my answer, 'Very sore.'

'I feared this would be the case. You have suffered trauma to your throat both internally and externally. You will need to drink your water regularly but start with small sips and gradually build up the size of your mouthfuls.' She helped me with another drink of water, then let me rest.

Another lady entered the room a few minutes later.

'Hello Phoebe, I am Dr. Stephany Brown. I need to do some tests now, is that okay?'

'Yes,' was my written reply.

She started by shining a torch in my eyes, then checked my reflexes. 'I need you to try standing up for me now. Do you think you can do this for me?'

I nodded.

'Good, okay now take your time and hang on to this walking frame if you need to.'

I shifted my legs to the edge of the bed and attempted to stand. So much of my body ached that I found this very challenging, but I persisted. Pulling myself up using the frame was possible, but I felt very dizzy and almost fainted.

'Okay, easy does it, Phoebe. You can sit down now.'

I was glad to plant myself firmly on the bed again.

'I would like to run some scans of your body and your head, Phoebe. These are routine for all people who present with your symptoms and in most cases, we don't find anything nasty, so there is no cause for alarm. I am going to go make the necessary arrangements, but in the meantime, I would like for you to continue drinking your water, okay?'

When she left the room, I was still sitting on the edge of the bed. This gave me the opportunity to take stock of my injuries. I had cuts and bruises all over my legs and arms, even my chest and belly. Gauze dressings covered some of the larger gashes. *What happened to me? Had I been in a car accident?*

Mum arrived soon after the doctor left the room. She took one look at me and teared up. 'Oh God, Phoebe. My sweet girl.' She moved up close and hugged me, which made me flinch due to the pain. 'Oh no, I'm sorry sweetie, did that hurt?'

I nodded.

Mr. Collins stepped forward and explained that I couldn't talk because of my throat injuries. 'Can I speak with you outside a moment, Laura?'

They both stepped out, along with the man known as Heath. I could hear a lot of talking but couldn't make out the details. Then Mum burst into tears. *What could have been so bad as to make her cry? What weren't they telling me?*

They stepped back into my room, where I had

settled back in my bed, beneath my blanket. Mum pulled up a chair close to me and gently took my hand.

We passed the time in silence for a while, then the doctor returned and wheeled me out of the room so that she could perform the scans. When I returned to my room, they were all waiting anxiously to hear what the doctor had to say.

She addressed us all. 'Well, the prognosis is generally positive from a physiological point of view. There are no infections or internal injuries aside from the throat, which I am certain will heal within a few days. There are no tumours or anything else medical that could be causing the amnesia. It is most likely the result of psychological trauma and possibly some loss of oxygen to the brain as suggested by the external throat trauma, although there is no permanent brain damage. Phoebe's memory should recover in time, especially if you all help her, but she is going to need some ongoing psychiatric treatment, especially when her memories of the traumatic events start to return.'

When Dr. Brown left, everyone, except for me, let out a huge sigh of relief. I still didn't fully understand what was going on, but I figured the news of my condition must have been good, so I forced a smile.

Chapter Thirty-Four

Diary extract dated Wednesday 27ᵗʰ February 2002

While a few details returned sooner, a lot of my memories came flooding back today, some of them painfully so, which was why I asked Denise to bring me this diary. I can finally remember Heath and the reasons why he and Jonah keep visiting me in the hospital. I recall Nick, although it wasn't until I read my diary entries and re-read his letter that I realised why he hasn't been to visit. It's been an emotionally draining day.

W hen Jonah and Heath called in to see me that Wednesday, I greeted them properly. I was able to talk again too, although my voice was croaky. 'Hi Jonah.'

This made him smile. 'Do you remember me properly now?'

'Yes, my love.'

He rushed to the side of my bed where he sat to hug and kiss me.

Then I smiled at Heath. 'Hi Heath.'

He returned the smile. 'Welcome back, Phoebe.' Heath sat down on the chair next to the bed.

I took a few large sips of water before proceeding. 'My memory is still quite fuzzy, but I am starting to piece things together. I need to ask you both some questions and I want you to be *completely* honest with me. Is that okay?'

They both nodded in agreement. I decided to start them with some test questions that I knew the answers to because of my diary. 'Where is Nick?'

They both shifted uncomfortably. Jonah answered this one. 'I'm sorry, Phoebe, but he moved to Sydney… without you... He found out about our affair… and ended your relationship.'

I teared up a little as the reality hit home again. 'Thank you, Jonah.' I turned to Heath. 'How well do we know each other, Heath?'

He blushed at this and avoided Jonah's gaze. 'Um, quite well… We've um… been very… intimate on one occasion.'

'Thank you, Heath.' Next came the difficult inquiries. 'Jonah, what happened between you and Sandra that day? Are the two of you back together?'

Heath appeared shocked by my question and looked at his dad accusingly.

'Oh my, heavens no! I would never take that witch back; no offence, Heath.'

'None taken, Dad,' Heath replied.

Jonah continued, 'Sandra called in to apologise for the blackmail that day. She confessed doing so partly out of jealousy because she wanted me back. She tried to manipulate her way into my bed, but I turned her away. I also berated her for speaking to you so cruelly.'

I breathed my own sigh of relief then. 'Thank you, Jonah. I'm sorry I doubted you.'

He kissed my cheek and whispered in my ear, 'That's okay. I'm sorry that I gave you so much cause for doubt.'

I drank some water, then continued, 'Now I need to fill in some gaps about my current condition.'

Both of their moods instantly shifted. It was like a large tempest filled the room. I knew something bad must have happened to cause the injuries I suffered, but I still had no idea what it was. Their reactions suggested something sinister. 'Who brought me into hospital?'

Heath sat on the opposite side of my bed to Jonah and said softly, 'We both brought you in, but I was the one that found you.'

'Where did you find me?'

He looked so downcast as he spoke. 'In the alley next to the *Private Cedar Lodge.*'

I thought about this for a few minutes, but still nothing came. 'How did you know to look for me there?'

'You were in trouble, and you rang me... although

according to what you said on the phone, you called from in the hotel. It was your… sobbing that alerted me to your whereabouts.'

Vague flashbacks started coming to me then. Memories of room 408, the ropes, the equipment. *The feeling of dread. Oh God, no!* I was so scared. I shuddered.

Jonah tried to comfort me by stroking my hair. 'Are you sure you want to do this now, Phoebe?'

I looked at him with tears in my eyes. 'Yes. Sorry Jonah, but I need to know.'

I turned back to Heath. 'What did I say to you on the phone?'

'You asked me for help. You told me your approximate location, being a hotel near *The Vault* nightclub. I assumed you'd come from there. You told me you had taken drugs, which was why you didn't want to call the police.' He paused to take a deep breath, then added, 'You told me they….' He gulped. 'R-raped you… and left you tied up. That was just before he returned.'

So that was it. The reason they were so hesitant to broach the topic. The reason for my injuries. The reason for my memory loss. I caught a mental glimpse of my attacker's face at the night club.

'Vince,' I whispered.

'What's that?' Jonah asked.

'He told me his name was Vince.'

I sensed Jonah's mood lift slightly then. 'That is a

promising sign. If you can remember him, perhaps the police will be able to catch him.'

'Maybe, but I have so little to go on.' I remembered more faces then… then more pain and I winced. 'There were two others as well.'

Jonah embraced me, holding me close as he stifled his own tears. 'Oh Phoebe. I am sorry they mistreated so. I hope we can bring those… *scumbags* to justice.'

That's when something else occurred to me. 'Oh God! They took my wallet and keys! They know where I live. I have to warn Mum!'

'Do not worry about that, Phoebe,' Jonah replied. 'When we found you without any of your personal belongings, we reported your attack to the police. They advised your mum to change the locks, which she did promptly before leaving the house. Unmarked patrol cars have been watching your place ever since. They are hoping the perpetrator will attempt a break-in soon, so that they can catch him.'

I relaxed a little, but worried about my own criminal actions coming to light. 'But if this was all reported to the police, will I get in trouble for drug use?'

'The hospital would have performed a drug test when you were admitted, to help with your treatment,' Heath explained. 'But those results are confidential, so I doubt the cops would have seen them. What did you use?'

'It was ecstasy that night. It would have been at

least a week since I tried anything else.'

Jonah gaped and fell silent.

Heath continued, 'Well the good news is that some forms of MDMA can be water soluble, so your drink could have been spiked with it. That's if the cops even bring it up.'

Jonah frowned at Heath. 'Your own knowledge of drugs worries me, son.' Then he turned to me. 'When did all this substance abuse start, Phoebe?'

I bowed my head in shame. 'Soon after I saw Sandra putting her hands all over you.'

'Oh Phoebe, I am so sorry! I never should have been so dismissive of you!' He sobbed.

'Please don't blame yourself, Jonah,' I insisted.

₭₩

Two female police officers came to see me later that day. After introducing themselves as Tania and Jacquie, Tania spoke, 'I hear that your memories have started to return, Phoebe. I know this must be a painful process for you, but we would like to ask you some questions so that we can help you, okay?'

'Okay,' I gulped.

They both sat down in chairs next to my bed. 'Are you able to tell us your own recollections of the events leading up to your admission into this hospital on Sunday 24th? Please take your time and try to avoid stating anything that you have been told if you do not actually remember it.'

Most of the details prior to my first blackout came to me easily. I still couldn't remember ringing Heath, or what followed and I omitted the drug use.

'You mentioned that you recognised this Vince fellow when you arrived at the nightclub? Where had you seen him before?'

I felt sick thinking back to the first time I encountered him. 'I met him at a private party, then I saw him at *The Vault* nightclub a couple of times again before *that* night.'

'Who hosted the party?'

'I don't know. I went with some old school friends. It was in one of the warehouses on the southern side of town.'

The two officers exchanged concerned glances. Tania continued, 'Would you be able to recognise the warehouse if you saw it again?'

This question struck me as odd. *What did that place have to do with my assault near the club?*

'Probably, but why?'

'Identifying any other places where you saw this man could help us track him down.'

That made sense, but I suspected something else was going on.

Tania concluded their visit by handing me her contact card. 'Thank you, Phoebe. We would like to speak with you further once you are out of hospital. Can you please come into the station and ask for me at your earliest convenience?'

I agreed to do so. I was keen to have those villains locked away.

My psychiatric treatment commenced immediately following the police interview. It was evident that I would need a lot of sessions, so the psychiatrist developed a long-term care plan for me. Having this in place meant that I was just about ready to leave the hospital, but they kept me in overnight so that Dr. Brown could see me one last time and approve my discharge papers.

It was good to arrive home at last. Mum was especially attentive for several days, which really helped with re-establishing a routine. The timing of this whole drama had been poor because I only had four days at home before I needed to start university and I missed all my orientation week! Luckily, Heath was able to attend several key events for me, so he filled me in. Mum suggested applying for leave, but I decided study would be a helpful way to get my mind off the horrible things that had happened. My physical injuries had healed well enough, and the amnesia did not interfere with my studies.

I also needed to catch up with Dad for his birthday—Friday 1st March—following my return home.

When he arrived at our meeting point, a favourite pasta restaurant of ours, he hugged me tighter than ever before. 'I'm so glad to see you looking healthy again. You had me so worried!'

'Hi Dad. I'm sorry. It's good to see you too. Happy Birthday!'

He smiled as we took our seats.

Then I added, 'I feel bad that I couldn't get you a gift in time.'

'Oh sweetheart, I'm not worried about any gifts. Just having you here is enough.'

With that, I smiled. It felt good to relax and enjoy a good meal with Dad again.

Chapter Thirty-Five

Diary extract dated Friday 15th March 2002

Why can't people understand that what Jonah and I feel for each other extends beyond all barriers, whether they be age, profession, or otherwise?

It felt good to immerse myself in the academic world again. It gave me a much-needed sense of control. I was also thankful for Jonah's support and understanding. He didn't attempt anything sexual because he wanted to be sure that I was ready, so he left that ball in my court. We grew closer during this time, bonding platonically through tender kisses, gentle touches, and long conversations.

I went to the police station for a follow up with Officer Tania during my first week at university. As part of this second interview, she asked me to make a formal statement then took me for a ride along the southern side of town to identify that warehouse.

The Crime Scene tape around the perimeter confirmed my original suspicions. Somehow my case intertwined with another.

'What happened here?' I asked.

'What didn't happen here would be an easier question to answer. I'm not privy to all the details, nor can I share all that I do know, but until recently, this building was crime HQ for many years. That party of yours was the last of its kind on this site. The drug squad raided just before dawn the following morning.'

I stared at her in amazement. 'I… I had no idea.'

'It's okay, Phoebe. You are not under any suspicions. They used those parties to coax other young girls, just like you. You were one of the lucky ones, I'm afraid.'

I shuddered at the thought of what happened to them, what might have become of me.

'It does mean that your assistance in identifying and catching your attackers has become even more critical.'

I nodded.

'Would you mind meeting with our sketch artist to build an identikit of these men?' Tania asked.

'I will do whatever I can to help.'

'Thank you, Phoebe.' She took me back to the station where I helped prepare three pictures of those men.

It was easy enough to bring Vince's face to mind,

but the other two were more difficult. My subconscious still blocked out much of what they had done to me, so all I had to go on were brief glimpses.

၈၁ဢ

It had become commonplace for me to visit Jonah each day after uni before heading home and that Friday was no different. At least not until I walked into my dining room. This was when I found Mum. She was staring at the table with tears streaming down her face and a look of disgust in her eyes. I followed her gaze and when I saw the photos I sank into a chair and prepared myself for reprimand. I trembled as I asked, 'Mum?'

She looked up at me and it seemed as though she only just registered my presence. 'Oh, my sweet girl! I'm not going to let him get away with abusing you like this.'

Oh God! She had the wrong idea entirely! 'No, Mum! He never… it was always consensual. I wanted him just as much.'

She blinked at me, unable to fathom what I was saying. 'Phoebe, he was your teacher! His authority over you must have been an influencing factor!'

'Not at all. He wasn't my teacher when we first hooked up. We all thought he was about to change schools.'

The shock on her face increased, giving her skin a

deathly pale hue. 'When did it start?'

'April last year. We tried to call things off when his transfer fell through, but our feelings for each other were too strong. We couldn't keep away from each other.'

She shook her head in astonishment. 'I can't believe what I'm hearing. Has he really deluded you this much?'

'I'm telling you Mum—he has done me no harm!'

'I'm not going to sit by and watch him destroy you, Phoebe. I forbid you from seeing this man anymore!'

I stood in a fit of rage then. *'Don't be ridiculous mum! I'm an adult now and I can date who ever I want!'*

She raised herself up to tower over me. *'How dare you speak to me like that! I am still your mother and while you live in my house with my support you will follow my rules! You will not date that man—do you hear me?'*

'Fine if that's how you want it—I will move out!'

She stared at me in stunned silence for a moment, then lowered her voice. 'You can't be serious!'

'Well I am!' I stormed out and ran to my bedroom where I quickly threw a few clothes along with my cash savings into my uni bag.

'Phoebe!' she called down that hall. I could hear her footsteps approaching.

I made my exit through the window seat into the courtyard, where I promptly left by the side gate. Running down the street as fast as I could, I heard her cry my name one last time before I was out of earshot. I went straight to Denise's house. When she answered the door, I hurried inside and collapsed to catch my breath.

'What's going on Phoebs? Are you okay?' Worry permeated her voice.

'Can you please drive me to Jonah's place? I will explain on the way.'

'Um, okay, but—'

'*Please Denise*, I promise to tell you, but we need to go *now*.' I knew it was only a matter of time before Mum caught up and I didn't want her to track me to his place.

'Okay, okay. Come on.'

Once we were safely away and I was sure that Mum wasn't following, I breathed a sigh of relief, then told Denise about the fight.

'Oh God, Phoebe. I'm sorry. So, Mr. C… I mean Jonah has invited you to live with him?' She was still struggling to comes to terms with the idea of me dating our former teacher and the name adjustment was just a part of it.

'Not exactly, I'm kinda hoping he will take me in.'

'Geez, hun, you're really tempting fate now.' I knew her heart was in the right place, but those words just made me feel more anxious.

When we arrived at Jonah's apartment, his eyes widened, and he jumped up to greet me. 'Phoebe? What happened?'

I dropped my bag and ran into his arms. Denise sat down in one of the armchairs and waited patiently. She wasn't going anywhere until she knew I had secured some accommodation.

I began to sob between my words of explanation. 'It's Mum… She found… She…'

He held me close and tried to reassure me, but his own unease made this a difficult task.

'Shh, everything will… be okay. Try to calm down a bit, then tell me.'

I cried for a while, then when I felt able to talk more comprehensibly, I said, 'Mum saw those photos. Sandra must have… We argued. She wanted me to stop seeing you… so I… ran away from home.'

'Oh, Phoebe! I… I am sorry.' He sat us down on the couch, refusing to release his hold of me in the process.

I looked into his eyes. 'Can I please live with you?'

He didn't hesitate to reply, 'Of course. But are you sure this is what you want? Living with me will be a big contrast to the home life you are used to and… things will feel different between us.'

'I'm sure.'

'If you are certain.' He looked at me closely, then smiled. 'Welcome to your new home.'

We embraced, then kissed deeply.

Denise coughing brought me back to the moment. 'Shall I leave you two lovebirds to it then?' she teased.

'Oh, sorry Denise. Um, thanks for helping me out.'

She stood up. 'It's all good. I'd best be going though. See ya, hun.'

I hugged her goodbye then returned to Jonah's arms.

Chapter Thirty-Six

Diary extract dated Monday 8ᵗʰ April 2002

The look of dismay on Jonah's face sent shivers down my spine. I knew something terrible must have happened.

I t took a little adjusting to my new living arrangements, especially residing with two men. My need for things to be neat and tidy was often at odds with my housemates, especially Jonah who liked his 'organised chaos.' But none of these disagreements were major and we got along well for the most part.

Mum made a few attempts to contact me, both directly and via my friends. I ended up sending her a message to assure her that I was safe and asked her to please respect my privacy. I didn't want to see her in person because I knew she wasn't going to accept Jonah as my partner, and I couldn't face her tirade.

Mondays were one of my short days at uni. I had a lot of work to go on with that day, so I decided to head straight home despite Heath's attempts to lure me to the pub.

I was surprised to see that Jonah was home from work early. He hunched over the dining table with a cup of tea. When he looked up at me, his eyes betrayed grief and I knew something was wrong. I dashed to comfort him, but he didn't respond to my touch. 'Jonah?'

'I'm ruined,' he said simply.

I searched his eyes for a clue, but nothing. 'Why? What happened?'

He didn't say anything but handed me a notice typed on the school's letterhead.

Attention Mr. Jonah Collins,

Following a recent complaint relating to inappropriate behaviour with a (now former) student of this school, an inquiry into your professional conduct is required. You are hereby officially suspended from teaching and prohibited from entering the school grounds pending this investigation. You will receive a written summons from the Teachers' Registration Board concerning this matter.

From,

Janice Caldwell

Oh God no! One of our greatest fears had reared its ugly head.

'I thought Sandra...' I stopped as I realised. 'It was Mum, wasn't it?'

He nodded.

I teared up and felt a lump in my throat. 'I'm so sorry, Jonah.' *Why had she done this? What did Mum think she would gain by reporting this?* I decided to find out just how much damage she had done. I went into the study and rang my mother.

'Phoebe is that you?'

'Yes.'

She breathed a sigh of relief. 'Oh, thank God. I was so worried about you. Are you okay?'

'Mum, I already told you I was safe and well. Now I am both upset and pissed. Why the hell did you go and report Jonah?'

There was silence on her end of the line for a minute. 'What he did to you was wrong, Phoebe. He must pay for acting so inappropriately. Where are you, sweetheart?'

I couldn't believe that she was still so deluded about my relationship with him. 'With Jonah.'

'Oh, God sweetie—is he holding you captive?'

'*No Mum*! We are very happy together. Well, we were happy before you went and ruined his career. Mum, can you please tell me how much you told the school? Did you give them the photos?'

It sounded like she was crying. 'Yes Phoebe. I gave them the photos and I told them that it had been going on since April last year.'

Shit! He really is ruined! 'Well *thank you* very much! If this is your sick way of trying to get me to return home, it isn't working! If anything happens to Jonah, I would rather live on my own than with you!' I hung up on her.

When I returned to Jonah, he was still in his almost catatonic state. The tea he had been cradling was cold. I took the cup from him and brewed another that I offered him. 'Here, this one's fresh.'

He looked at me then at the tea. 'Thank you, Phoebe.'

This time he drank it, then sighed before forcing a smile that did little to hide his anguish. 'Well, done is done I suppose. I am going to bed.'

'But it's only one o'clock! What about dinner and stuff?' I asked.

'I'm not hungry, just tired. You can join me later if you feel so inclined.' He shuffled off to the bedroom, leaving me alone in my own melancholy.

After sitting in silent gloom for a while I decided to snap myself out of it and get on with my study. Then after a take-away dinner with Heath, I curled up in bed next to Jonah and held him close.

෧෬

The summons came a week later, and they gave

Jonah a month's notice to prepare for the hearing. In the meantime, Jonah had just moped about the apartment, eating little and saying even less. I was also beckoned to give evidence. They probably thought I was a victim based on Mum's attitude to the whole thing. I decided I would go and try to argue Jonah's case.

It was tense waiting for the trial. I could feel Jonah slipping away from me and at one stage he even snapped at me. 'None of this would have happened if you handled things better with your damn mother!'

I was already in a foul mood myself that day, having spent half the day cleaning up his mess of dirty dishes and laundry, so I retorted, 'Well you wouldn't be in this mess if you'd kept your hands off me in the first place!'

His expression was one of utter astonishment and pain.

I broke down and cried my apology, 'Oh God, Jonah! I... I didn't mean that. I... I'm so sorry!'

He just stared at me coldly and stormed off into the bedroom, slamming the door shut behind him.

I slumped down on the couch.

Heath, having witnessed the whole incident, sat next to me. 'Geez Phoebe, that was pretty harsh.'

I continued to sob. 'I... I know. I really didn't... mean to. It's just been so hard... the way he keeps shutting me out. I feel... so lonely.'

'I know Phoebe, I'm sorry. This has been a tough time for all of us.' He reached out his arms, and I accepted his embrace.

As we started to pull away from each other, I looked into his eyes. We remained locked in one another's gaze for a moment. It had been a few weeks since I had felt a warm touch or a tender kiss from Jonah and I had not ventured out into anyone else's bed since Vince attacked me. At that moment I realised just how much I had missed and needed intimate contact, so I leaned in and kissed him.

He yielded.

With the feel of his soft yet demanding lips pressed against mine, I felt a rush of desire through my body for the first time in almost two months. My hand drifted across the tent forming in Heath's pants, eliciting a groan from him. 'Can we take this to your bedroom?'

'Fuck! I know I shouldn't, but I just can't resist you, Phoebe.' Heath tugged me out of the couch and drew me into his room.

80C8

I felt happy again the following day. Heath and I woke up and got ready for uni together. It just so happened that we had two lectures and a tutorial in common that day, so it was a good opportunity to stay close to each other. The tutorial was for philosophy and the discussions that arose in class often got us talking for some time afterwards. The hot topic of the moment was taboos. This was the foundation of our major assignment and I had chosen to focus on sexual taboos.

After the tutorial, we went to the uni pub. Heath ordered the first round: beer for himself, and since I never could abide the taste of that stuff, I asked for a cider.

Sitting down with our drinks, I asked, 'Okay Heath, what's your opinion on incest?'

'Oh wow—that's a tricky one. What type of incest are we talking here?'

'Any form. Society outlaws sex between any first-degree and even second-degree relatives, right? It doesn't matter what the age gap is, so consenting siblings would still be breaking the law. But people even frown upon cases of incest with more distant relatives or step relatives.'

He sat back and sipped his drink while he thought. 'Hmm... well I don't have a problem with people related by marriage alone doin' it. Heck, you are practically my step-mother and well, you know what I think of sex with you.' He gave me a lecherous grin, which made me laugh.

'You make it seem so dirty when you put it that way. But seriously though, what would you think of two consenting siblings having sex?'

'I'd think, *ick!*'

'Why is that?'

He paused for thought. 'I guess that'd be because I've been brought up to think that way. Society teaches us that incest is bad.'

'That, there, is the crux of the matter.'

'But what about the increased odds of deformed babies?'

'Sex isn't just a means for having kids. I'm not suggesting that siblings should reproduce.'

I left him to ponder that while ordering the second round of drinks. When I returned, I inquired, 'What *do you* think of sex with me?'

He leaned in close to respond, 'What—here and now? It's a bit public, don't you think?'

I laughed then nudged him with my elbow. 'I mean what goes through your mind when you contemplate sex with me?'

'There doesn't tend to be a lot of higher brain function involved when it comes to sex.'

'Well sure, when it comes to the act, but if you sit back for a moment and actually think about it, what then?'

He did just that. 'You sure you want to know?'

My turn to grin.

He leaned forward again. 'Okay, well I think things like "Hmm Phoebe is really hot, just looking at her right now makes me hard" and "I would so love to bend that girl over right now and take her from behind," or when I think back to last night, I have thoughts like "damn, that was some of the best sex I've ever had." Shall I go on?'

I was blushing profusely by this point. 'That's enough—thank you Heath.'

'Alright Phoebe. What do *you* think of sex with me?'

Oh God! It was a difficult question to answer when I thought about it. I decided to be cheeky instead. 'I think we should go home and do it right now.'

He didn't need any more encouragement. Grabbing my hand, he led me straight out of the pub, our drinks left half-full. Jonah was out when we got home (probably at a meeting with his lawyer), so we headed straight for Heath's room.

We both got so caught up in the fun and intensity of our experience that we didn't hear the front door. It would have been hard to hear much of anything above my own screaming, although I did hear my phone ringing just in time to miss the call. It was in my bag, which I had dropped beside the bed. I checked the missed call log. 'It was your dad,' I said.

Heath's phone rang next. We looked at each other then he checked the incoming call. 'It's Dad. Hang on, I'll put him on loudspeaker... Hi Dad what's—'

'You ought to know that I am standing outside your bedroom door. I will give you both one minute to put some clothes on, then I am coming in.'

He hung up.

Shit! I was planning to tell him, but I really wish he hadn't found out this way. I threw my dress on, then sat back on the bed just in time.

The door opened. Jonah had been very depressed lately, but the look on his face when he entered was next-level misery. He sat at the end of the bed. 'Heath, we both know that you could bed any girl you wanted. Why do you have to go and take mine?'

'Well firstly, you never said that Phoebe and I couldn't do it. Secondly, you know how hot she is. How I am supposed to resist her when you couldn't?' It felt so awkward hearing them talk about me when I was right there.

Jonah closed his eyes for a moment. When they reopened, I could see that he was suppressing tears. He turned to me. 'Phoebe, I have not forgotten our agreement, but I had hoped your first time following *that* incident would at least be with me. Why did you turn to Heath and not me?'

'Because you kept shutting me out, Jonah. You weren't there for me when I was ready and in need.'

His eyes closed again. When they opened, he looked remorseful. 'I am sorry Phoebe. I… I was not myself.' His tears started to flow.

I moved to him and curled up in his lap. 'I'm sorry too, Jonah.'

ℰℭ

In the final week leading up to the hearing, Jonah was incredibly tense, but his reclusive behaviours had eased up and we were able to comfort each other.

When questioned by the panel of investigators, I told them the truth of the matter. I didn't give them any gritty details, but I explained how I felt about Jonah and that he did not employ any undue influence. I also put a point to them for consideration. 'I have a question for all of you now. Given that I was old enough to consent to sex with Jonah, and the fact that he never let our relationship influence his treatment of my academic work, what was so wrong with us being intimately involved?'

They were all surprised by what I said and shifted uncomfortably in their seats. I guessed they weren't used to students, or even former students, challenging them like this. One of them concluded the interview, 'Thank you, Miss Braddock. That will be all.'

Another week of waiting. Jonah was more anxious and restless than before. Not a great time for Sandra to show up. It was in the evening and all three of us were home watching television. Heath opened the door. 'Mum? What the hell are you doing here?'

She hugged him briefly, then barged her way into the apartment. 'I've come to see you, Heath. Can I not see my own son?'

I glared at her with open hatred. Jonah rose to challenge her, but Heath intervened, 'Of course you can see me, Mum—just not here. Come on, let's get a coffee.' He grabbed her arm and led her outside.

He returned an hour later. 'Well Dad, I think I have managed to convince Mum to stay out of your personal life. She's been offered a job in the United States, and I encouraged her to take it.'

Jonah smiled. 'That is some of the best news I have heard in a long time. Thank you, Heath.'

This was a relief, but it didn't undo the damage she had already done. I thought about the impact of Sandra's actions on my relationship with my own mother. I was still angry with Mum, but I was also beginning to miss her. I resolved to visit her once I had a chance to calm down after the inquiry was over.

Jonah's lawyer, Connor, delivered the news. It was a Monday afternoon, and I was home at the time. Connor suggested moving into Jonah's study for privacy, but Jonah wanted me present, so we all sat in the lounge area.

Connor spoke in a very formal tone. 'I have the decision of the board here in writing. They are stripping you of your current registration. You may not reapply until you have completed professional conduct training.' His tone relaxed. 'No fine, no prison, no permanent disqualification. So, that's it my friend.'

He handed Jonah a copy of the written notice. Jonah let out an audible sigh of relief. 'Thank you, Connor.'

Connor smiled at us both then. 'Just doing my job.

You really ought to thank your girlfriend here. I think she did a lot to save your skin.' He must have been referring to what I'd said in my interview. I remembered seeing him there at the time.

As soon as he had gone, Jonah flung his arms around me. 'Thank you, Phoebe.'

We kissed with renewed vigour.

ℰᏇ

If I were writing one of my own fictional stories, I might have ended things there—or soon after— giving the impression of a happily ever after; but real life doesn't work that way.

Chapter Thirty-Seven

Diary extract dated Thursday 11th July 2002

'So, Heath, word round here is you like to watch. That true?'

Heath went pale as he replied, 'Yes, but...'

'Nice. I sense a kindred spirit in you, Heath. We might've been friends if we'd met under different circumstances.'

Heath grimaced, then said bluntly, 'I doubt that.'

I paid Mum a visit soon after Jonah received his notice. When the door opened, she threw her arms around me. I hesitated at first, but then I returned the embrace, albeit lightly.

With a hopeful tone Mum asked, 'Are you moving back?'

I sighed out of frustration. 'No Mum. Just visiting.'

Her enthusiasm plummeted. In a disappointed

tone she continued, 'Well at least you haven't forgotten me entirely. Come in.'

I sat down in the family room while she made tea. 'So, Jonah's teaching career is safe. He's only briefly suspended until he has done some special training. We were both relieved.'

No comment.

I went on, 'I spent some time thinking and I've decided to forgive you.'

Still nothing, not even a look of acknowledgement. She wasn't going to make this easy.

'I'm sorry Mum.'

She poured our tea and looked up then. I could see tears in her eyes. I walked into the kitchen and gave her a hug. Her reply came through sobs, 'Oh Phoebe... I was... so worried! I've missed you.'

The impact of what I'd put her through hit me then and I broke down myself. We just cried together for a bit, then took our cups of tea to the couch. 'I've missed you too Mum.'

'Why don't you come home then?' she pleaded.

'Because I'm happy with Jonah.'

She sipped her tea quietly for a moment. 'I don't know what to do without you, Phoebe.'

'I'll still see you. It's not like I've moved to the other side of the world. I... didn't even go to Sydney.'

Mum looked around the room, then back at me. 'This house... it's so big for just one.'

So that was the problem. 'Well on the plus side, you can bring whoever you want home.'

She smiled at last. 'Yes, I guess you're right.'

The conversation shifted to lighter topics then and I left the place feeling much better.

෪෬

My social life improved considerably during the months following the end of Jonah's inquiry. We were all in a better mood and I felt relaxed enough to start partying again. However, safety was still at the forefront of my mind, so I only ever went with a male friend I could trust as a chaperone. This was usually Heath, although when Denise joined me, Curtis would sometimes be the one I asked to watch my back.

We occasionally went to night clubs, although I avoided *The Vault* at all costs. Most of the time we hung out at the uni pub or private parties. I even returned to exploring my sexuality, but I maintained control of my senses and my situation.

During the mid-year break Heath and I attended a birthday party for Rebecca, one of our Philosophy friends. The house—an enormous white-stone Georgian mansion—sat just outside of the city centre. I knew Rebecca was from a wealthy family, but I was not expecting such a grand building to be her home. Apparently, it had been in her family for as long as it had stood.

After a little conversation with the core group, Heath made his way outside to smoke while I mingled with the crowd for a few hours. I never expected him to hold my hand when we were out; it was enough for me to know that he was nearby.

It happened when I returned to the central area, having just grabbed myself a drink: I looked across the room and recognised a face that made me freeze with dread. He saw me too, grinning as he did so. When he began to move towards me, I quickly gathered my senses and looked around for Heath. He wasn't back inside yet, so I escaped out the back to track him down. I followed my nose to find the stoners, calling out, 'Heath?'

'No Heath here babe, but I'd make ya happy,' said one guy with a giggle.

He wasn't inside drinking, or outside smoking drugs. Perhaps he was partaking of his other favourite vice. I ran back inside and headed upstairs, catching a glimpse of my pursuer as I did. *Shit, most of the bedrooms were occupied!* I was going to have to try them all. I opened the first door to reveal a group of two couples, but I couldn't see their faces. 'Heath?'

They all looked at me surprised. No Heath. One of the girls smiled, 'Not here, sorry hun. But why don't you join us?'

Under normal circumstances I might have considered it, but this time I just shut the door and moved on. The next few rooms were just straight couples. They did not yield Heath, just some angry glares and shouts. My stalker reached the landing then, so I ducked into the nearby bathroom and locked the door.

My heart was pounding so hard that I wondered if it would burst. I sat on the chair next to the spa bath and grabbed my phone out of my bag. I could hear him trying the door and fumbled with the phone, dropping it on the tiles. *Shit!* As I reached for it, the door swung open, breaking the lock. I sprang to my feet—luckily with phone in hand.

He continued that God-awful smile. 'Hello Phoebe, long time no see.'

'Back off Vince! I *will* call the cops this time!'

Moving into the room, he closed the door and leaned against it. 'If you do, you and all your weed-smoking friends would go down with me.'

He spoke so calmly, it made me sick. His point was valid though. It didn't matter that I wasn't consuming the stuff; just being around the drugs would get me in trouble. Vince moved close enough to touch my face with his vile hand.

'What the hell are you doin' here Vince? This party's invite only!'

'Oh sweet, naïve Phoebe. Where do think the Birthday Girl gets all her drugs from?' His other hand moved to the hem of my skirt, so I tried to push it away, but he just grabbed my wrist instead. 'You've become a feisty fucker. I kinda miss easy

Phoebe.' He grabbed my other hand and pushed me against the wall. 'But that's okay cos I can still enjoy a good fight before a hard fuck.'

I kneed him hard between the legs and broke free of his grip, then made for the door.

Vince wasn't so easily defeated, however, because he caught the hood of my jacket and pulled me back into his arms, laughing. 'Stupid girl. Don't you think I'd be used to whores' tricks by now and protect myself?'

My God—this man was so cold and calculating! All I could think to do was scream as loud as possible, '*Heath!*'

I struggled in his arms while he continued sniggering. 'You really think that soft-arse boyfriend of yours can save you?' he teased.

Heath's reply came from down the hall. '*Phoebe? Where are you?*'

Vince tried to cover my mouth with one of his hands, but I bit it hard and cried, '*Bathroom!*'

'Oh, you dirty cunt. You want a threesome, do you?' Vince retorted.

At that point I saw him produce a pistol and point it at the door. *Oh God, I've put Heath's life at risk!* I couldn't hold back the tears any longer.

He burst through the door, wearing nothing but his jeans. 'Phoebe, What's wr...' He froze in the doorway when he saw the gun pointed at him.

I sobbed as I tried to explain, 'This is... Vince.'

'Heath, I presume? It's *so nice* to finally meet you. I think we spoke briefly on the phone a few months back.'

Heath remained silent, unable to move.

Vince went on, 'Now just so we're clear, any false moves and one of you *will* get shot. See that empty room across the hall, Heath? Slowly turn around and enter it. We'll be right behind you.'

Heath followed his instructions.

We walked into an empty bedroom and Vince closed the door behind us. Then he pointed the gun at me and pushed me towards the bed. 'Make yourself comfortable Phoebe,' he demanded.

I sat back on the bed, dreading what else he would expect me to do. Vince locked the door somehow using a fork. Then he turned and pointed the gun at Heath again. 'So, Heath, word round here is you like to watch. That true?'

Heath went pale. 'Yes, but—'

'Nice. I sense a kindred spirit in you, Heath. We might've been friends if we'd met under different circumstances.'

With a grimace, Heath replied bluntly, 'I doubt that.'

Vince feigned injury. 'Oh, such a blow. You hurt my feelings, Heath. Never mind, I'm the forgiving sort. I wanted to treat you to a special show tonight. Take a seat.'

Oh God no!

Pointing to the nearby chair, Vince returned the gun to his belt and pulled out a knife. Heath slowly sat down. Vince advanced on me with the knife, and I started having flash backs of his first attack. 'Lose the jacket, Phoebe,' he insisted.

I hesitated at first, but then he knelt beside me and pressed the knife to my throat. After I complied with his demand, he cut my blouse open, buttons spraying across the room, revealing my corset. Vince was briefly distracted by the sight, giving Heath a window of opportunity. He jumped up, grabbed the chair he was on and struck Vince hard against the back of the head with it, knocking him unconscious.

Heath and I dashed for the exit, but we struggled with the makeshift lock, which lost us precious time. Vince came to just in time to see us fleeing through the door. His gun fired.

I heard a series of loud screams around me as people came running out of the other rooms. Heath began to limp as we pushed through the crowd. I heard another shot and the people around us dispersed, many retreating to their rooms.

We made it to the stairs, but Heath was struggling and that was when I noticed the blood drops along the floor. I looked back and saw Vince stumbling along the hall towards us, pistol in hand, eyes wild.

Heath grabbed me and screamed, '*Drop and slide!*'

I followed his lead and we both glided down the wide, spiralling wooden staircase. We got a few startled looks and cries from the throng below, but I was beyond caring. Knowing that I needed to act fast to staunch Heath's bleeding, I considered using my jacket, but a quick inspection reminded me how scantily clad I was. I seized a nearby scarf, abandoned on the sofa next to me. I found the wound on the side of Heath's thigh and bandaged it. Then we dashed out the front door and up the gravel path, ducking behind a hedge.

I wanted to stop for a bit to check on Heath, but when we heard the door, followed by footsteps behind us, he whispered, 'Come on, we have to find a safe hiding spot before we stop.'

When we reached the street, Heath pulled us into some thick shrubs that concealed us well. I held him close to me for comfort and warmth. We both sat completely quiet and still. Vince approached the bushes and looked around, but he failed to detect us and moved on. Once he was a safe distance up the street, I breathed a sigh of relief, then called Officer Tania from my mobile.

'Tania speaking.'

I spoke as quietly as possible, finding it hard to control the anxiety in my voice, 'Tania—it's Phoebe Braddock. Vince is here. Please help!'

'Okay, try to stay calm Phoebe. Where are you?'

I explained my location and the direction that Vince had taken, then I asked, 'Can you send an ambulance? My friend Heath clobbered him, but

Vince shot him in the leg.'

'Yes, of course. Is he still conscious?'

Heath was sitting between my outstretched legs with his head resting against my chest. His eyes were closed, so I began to fear the worst. 'Heath? Are you still with me?' I whispered into his ear.

'Uh huh.'

I put the phone back to my ear. 'Yes, he is, but he's lost a lot of blood.'

'Don't move, I'll be right there with help.' Tania signed off.

Heath was shivering. It was a cold night and I worried that he would suffer from exposure. I wrapped my arms around him as much as I could, then kissed the top of his head.

He spoke blearily, 'If I perish here tonight, at least I will be between the legs of my favourite woman.'

The significance of what he said was not lost on me and I felt tears in my eyes. 'Shh! Don't talk like that Heath! You're not allowed to die on me! Not here, not like this.'

By the time the ambulance arrived Heath had drifted off. I could still feel a faint pulse, so I knew he was alive, for the time being.

ഇരു

I rang Jonah from the hospital.

'Is everything okay, Phoebe?' The late hour of my call must have alarmed him.

'I'm at the hospital—it's Heath.'

'Oh God! Is he okay?'

I started to cry. 'I… I don't know.'

'I am coming straight over.' He did just that. Being walking distance from the hospital proved advantageous. When he arrived, he hurried to embrace me. Then he noticed my lack of attire and promptly surrendered his woollen coat. 'What happened, Phoebe?'

I attempted an explanation between sobs. 'It was Vince… He… tried to… hurt me again… Heath intervened… Vince… shot him.'

'Shot him? Where?' Jonah's voice betrayed panic.

'His thigh.'

We sat down on one of the couches, Jonah holding me tight while we waited silently for news.

Officer Tania Brown found us in the meantime. She sat next to me. 'Hi Phoebe. How is he?'

'I don't know yet.' I sobbed.

She paused for a moment. 'When you see him, please thank him for us. We caught Vince thanks to Heath's concussive blow.'

Thank God! At least I didn't have to worry about the bastard coming after us again.

'I will leave you to it for now, but please come and see me at the station when you're ready, okay?

I nodded.

When the doctor approached us hours later, we rose, but Jonah didn't let me out of his arms.

The doctor observed our closeness and questioned Jonah with a hint of acumen and contempt in his tone, 'Sorry, but who might you be?'

Jonah replied with equal umbrage. 'Jonah Collins, Heath's father.'

The doctor seemed surprised and conceded, 'My apologies. I didn't realise.'

Jonah brushed off the doctor's scorn and asked the pressing question on both our minds, 'How is my son, doctor?'

'Heath is stable and conscious. We removed the bullet easily. There's no nerve damage, so with the right rehab he should be walking unaided in several months. We also put a drainage tube in his thigh to help reduce infection.'

I breathed easily again when he finished talking. 'Can we see him?'

'Yes but keep it brief. He needs rest.'

Heath's eyes lit up when we entered the room.

'Hi Heath. How do you feel?' I asked.

'Like I've been shot in the leg,' he said playfully.

I chuckled a little, but my mood became serious again when Jonah spoke. 'Heath, when Phoebe mentioned what you did, I was unsure whether to chide you or reward you for your bravery... Thank you.'

Heath blushed a little, then attempted to dismiss it with modesty. 'Ah, it was nothing. I'm sure you would have done the same, Dad.'

I smiled again. 'They caught him, Heath. That jerk is done for.'

'Good. I hope they put him away for life!'

'With his long list of felonies, I'm sure they will.' I could see him starting to drift off to sleep then, so I moved in close to bid him a whispered farewell, 'See you again soon, Heath.'

Then I kissed him on the forehead and Jonah followed suit.

Chapter Thirty-Eight

Diary extract dated Friday 12th July 2002

I was walking down a dark corridor in the hospital towards Heath's room. I thought it was odd that the backup generator had not kicked in when the lights blacked out. When I reached him, he was sleeping peacefully. I sat down on the bedside and put my hand on his cheek, recoiling instantly at the icy cold touch. Promptly, I checked his pulse. Nothing! I jumped up in a panic and tried to buzz for a nurse, but all was in vain due to the power outage. I ran out into the hallway. Where was everyone? I screamed out, 'Help, please somebody help!'

Nothing but silence. But then I caught a glimpse of movement down the hall. I moved towards it and was briefly relieved to see Jonah. 'It's Heath-come quick!'

But Jonah said nothing. He just slumped forward

to the floor, revealing the grinning face of Vince and the knife in Jonah's back.

...

I awoke sweating, my heart beating fast. It's rare for my dreams to be so vivid, but I will never forget this one.

Jonah was busy with his training the next day, so I called in to the hospital on my own. It was good to see Heath sitting up in bed. He was watching television at the time but switched it off as soon as I entered. 'Hey Phoebe.'

'Hi Heath. How's the leg today?'

I leaned in to kiss him on the cheek, but he pulled me down on the bed and kissed me properly. 'Now that's a proper greeting.' He grinned.

I stared at him in stunned silence for a moment.

'The leg feels like crap, but they have pretty good drugs here that help.'

I smiled as I regained my composure. 'Well that's something at least. How's the entertainment?' I gestured towards the television.

'Pretty dull really. Wouldn't mind some decent reading material.'

'I'll bring you some books from your room next time then.'

'Thanks, but... I'd still prefer your company to

any of it.'

This sent me into quiet contemplation for a while. 'Heath?' I asked apprehensively.

'Yes'm?'

'The other night when... we were hiding from him... you said something... Do you remember?'

He closed his eyes and tried to think. 'A lot happened that night, Phoebe. It might be hard for me to recall everything. Can you help me out here?'

I wondered if he was really struggling with his memory, if he enjoyed drawing this out, or if he had some other motive. 'You were... sitting between my legs at the time and... you said something about... perishing there that night.'

Realisation dawned on his face. 'Yes, that's right. I think I was feeling quite fatalistic at the time.'

'Did you really... mean the rest?'

He gripped my hand and looked straight into my eyes. 'You ought to know by now that I always speak my mind.'

My heart was racing. 'Does that mean you...' I trailed off, unable to put what I wanted to ask into words.

'Yes,' he assured me. Then he leaned in and kissed me again.

'Ahem,' came a woman's voice at the door. I turned to see a nurse entering the room. 'Sorry to interrupt, but I need some time with Heath here.'

I left the room to give the nurse the space she

needed. Leaning back against the wall just outside the door, I took a moment to process my feelings. I really should have seen this coming, given the chemistry between us combined with the way our friendship had been developing. But then does anyone ever really see it coming before it hits them? What did this mean for my relationship with Jonah? My feelings for him were still strong and I couldn't bear the thought of leaving him. I resolved to tell Jonah about my feelings for Heath when I got home that night.

The nurse left Heath's room, so I returned to him and spent the rest of the afternoon enjoying his company.

Jonah's favourite way to spend a cold winter's night generally involved curling up on the couch with a good book. It just so happened that this was also my favourite option, which was why we spent many a night reading on the couch together. He would sit cross-legged at one end of the couch, one arm around me as I stretched out and rested my head in his lap. We usually read our own books in silence this way, but occasionally when I was reading something Jonah was familiar with, I would start conversing with him about various issues raised by the author.

That Friday night started as such, with *Lady Chatterley's Lover* by D.H. Lawrence. Having just read about Connie's own realisation, I put the book down in my lap and sighed. Jonah must have anticipated a literary discussion about to start, so he put his paperback aside and queried, 'How goes the reading? You have not spoken to me at large on this one yet.'

'Oh, the book's okay, although it still amazes me that it was once banned as pornography when you compare it to what's readily available now. It's hard to fathom living in such as repressed society!'

He smiled. 'Indeed. Although I think our own is still too much of a cage for you.' That made me laugh a little. He was right though. 'So, what made you breathe that heavy sigh of yours?'

It was time to be honest. 'Connie's feelings have reminded of something... personal... I need to talk to you about.'

'Oh?' His expression changed to one of mild apprehension.

'Before I get to the point, I want you to know that I have always been completely honest with you about who I go to bed with and when.' His countenance was displaying more trepidation, making it harder for me to come out with it.

'I also want you to know that my feelings for you have not lessened. It's just that...'

'Yes?' he prompted me.

'Well... I have grown... extremely fond of someone else too.'

His head drooped as he mumbled, 'I see.'

The silence that followed was more excruciating. He eventually broke it, 'This was exactly what I feared would happen when I agreed to open our relationship!'

'Please Jonah,' I pleaded, 'I don't want this to come between us. I still want you.'

'How is that possible? Surely you are going to want to see this other lover more, maybe even live with him—or is this a woman?'

It appeared that he did not even suspect the full truth of the matter. 'But I already do.'

This confused him at first. 'You already do what?'

'Live with him,' I said.

It took a moment, but when my meaning registered, he went deathly pale and sat there in shock. I knew that he had always been uncomfortable with the idea of me and Heath being intimate, which was why I tended to avoid letting the flirting go too far on most occasions. It had only happened once since the time Jonah confronted us in bed and, as with all my other lovers, I had been upfront about it.

'Is it mutual?' he eventually asked.

'Yes... After talking with him today... and... the kiss we had... I'm sure.'

He stood up and paced the room. I was beginning to worry that this news would mean the end of our relationship. Tears were forming in my eyes. 'Jonah?'

'Sorry Phoebe, but this is a lot for me to take in.

Please give me some time and space.' With that he went off to the bedroom and closed the door.

Knowing that I would not be welcome in my own bed tonight, I found a fragment of comfort by curling up on Heath's mattress, breathing in his scent from the quilt. Sleep did not come easily; I needed to tire myself out weeping first, even then nightmares of losing them both plagued me.

೪೦೦೪

Jonah had already left the house by the time I awoke the next day. I found a note on the kitchen bench

Sorry Phoebe, but I need more time to think. Please find alternative accommodation until I contact you.

Shit! It was worse than I thought! I packed a few of my things, struggling to see through wet eyes, then called Denise.

'Hey Phoebs, how ya doin'?'

I sobbed into the phone. 'I need... a place... to crash... for a bit.'

'Oh God, hun what's wrong?'

'I'll explain... later. Can I stay... with you?'

She was still living at home, but I was on good terms with her parents, so I figured it would be fine with them. 'Yes, of course. I'll be right over.' It took her about an hour, which gave me enough time to shower and calm my nerves.

I told her about what happened when we were in the car.

'I'm sorry babe. I hope he doesn't take too long to think it over. I mean, you're welcome to stay as long as you like, but I know how painful it can be to wait, not knowing.'

'Thanks, hun.' I knew Denise was referring to her recent break with Curtis, which happened as a result of her making her own full-fledged bisexual persuasion known and asking for the freedom to explore this with other women. It took him a few weeks to come around to the idea, leaving her wondering if their relationship was entirely over. Later, when they did eventually get back together things really heated up for them.

That afternoon I called into the hospital again to see Heath. At least I knew how *he* felt.

When I arrived, I found Jonah with him. I hesitated to enter, but then Jonah saw me.

He stood up. 'Come in, Phoebe. I was just leaving.' And with that he was gone. He didn't even look me in the eyes as he left.

When I approached Heath, his brow furrowed. 'Wow that's the iciest chill I've felt in long time. What's up with you and Dad?'

I sat on the edge of his bed. 'You mean he didn't tell you?'

'Nope. I figured he was just his usual surly self.'

I sighed, unsure whether I should tell him yet.

He gripped my hand tightly and drew my face close to his. 'C'mon Phoebe, you know you can tell me anything.'

Tears began to trickle down my cheeks. 'I'm worried it's over between your dad and me.'

'Why? What happened?'

I bit my lip, then looked into his eyes. 'Us.'

He appeared confused. 'But how... why? He's known about us for ages.'

'I told him about our kiss yesterday.'

'I still don't understand how... Oh, I see.' He pulled me in close to rest his forehead against mine, then whispered, 'I'm sorry Phoebe. I never meant for this... for us to...' Then he kissed me deeply.

After the kiss, I began to sob harder and he held me tight.

'I'll try to talk Dad around to accepting it, 'kay?'

'Thanks Heath,' I mumbled.

I spent the rest of the visit just sitting quietly in his arms.

Jonah rang me a week later. Heath had returned home a couple of days after I told him about the issue, which meant I couldn't even visit him during the latter half of that week. So, I was biding my time in a sort of mournful dread. I was very thankful that Denise did not judge my lack of hygiene during this time because I would often hang around in my pyjamas most—if not all—of the day, and shower infrequently. The highlight of those days was the nightly phone call from Heath, which he made once Jonah was asleep.

When I saw that the caller was Jonah, my heart leaped into my throat, making talking almost impossible. ''Ello,' I stuttered.

'Phoebe?'

Hearing his voice again evoked a storm of emotions. 'Yes?'

'Please come home.'

They were the three little words that I most needed to hear. 'Really?' I asked, not quite sure I heard him right.

'Yes, really. I want to talk about… things, but not on the phone.'

My heart sank again. *He just wanted to talk?* That could mean anything. 'I'm sorry Jonah, but if you want to end things, I don't think I can bear to see you in person to hear it, so you'd better tell me now.'

He paused for a few seconds, but it felt like an eternity. 'I do not want to end our relationship, Phoebe. I want you back, but things are complicated now, so we need to talk them through.'

The relief I felt came gushing out of me, like a river breaking through flood gates. All I could do was reply, 'Okay.'

Then I hung up and rushed into the loungeroom, where I found Denise giving herself a pedicure.

My appearance startled her. 'My God, Phoebs! What is it?'

'Please take me home! *He wants me back!*' I shrieked through my tears with delight.

She jumped up, almost slipping with her wet feet as she rushed to embrace me. 'Oh, thank God! Okay—ok... Just give me a sec to get sorted.'

Before long I was back in Jonah's welcoming arms, kissing him madly. 'I missed you so much!'

'I have missed you too, Phoebe,' he acknowledged warmly.

As Jonah released me from his arms, I saw Heath hobbling out of his bedroom with crutches. He sat at the dining table and looked at me endearingly. I wanted to embrace him too, but I hesitated, unsure of Jonah's feelings. Jonah must have sensed this because he encouraged me. 'Go on, Phoebe. I do not mind.'

Wow! What a change from the Jonah I'd spoken to just over a week ago.

I pulled a chair up next to Heath and greeted him with a proper kiss. 'How's the leg?'

'It's healing okay, but aches to high heaven.'

I grimaced at the thought of what he was going through.

Jonah joined us then. 'At the risk of sounding rude, I think we should move on to the more pressing matter at hand.'

'Yes, of course. Sorry Jonah,' I replied.

He took a deep breath. 'I have given the whole situation a lot of thought. I have also spoken to Heath at length about it, so I have come to terms with the idea of the two of you and what that means as far as I am concerned.' He paused briefly to clear his throat before venturing on to say, 'I am also conscious of our age gap, Phoebe, which may not seem like a problem to you now, but I am reminded of it every time you are off socialising without me. I do not want to stop you enjoying your youth, which is why I am happy for you to have this freedom.' Again, he paused, and I looked at him in anticipation. 'What I am trying to say is that I would feel a lot better about you going out at night with Heath... as your boyfriend, not just as a chaperone, because I can trust him more than anyone else.'

Heath gripped my hand tight at that moment and I squeezed his in response.

'But what about us?' I inquired of Jonah.

'I do not see a need for things between us to differ much. One thing that I would like to insist upon, though, is that when we are at home together, I want you to join me at bedtime first before spending time in Heath's bed. Is that okay with you?'

I was amazed at how accepting he had become. I replied excitedly, 'Yes, of course.'

He smiled then. 'Thank you, Phoebe. Outside of the bedroom, I think that we can all continue to enjoy each other's company freely as we have been doing thus far.'

Heath spoke up then. 'Something else just occurred to me, Dad. What about PDAs?'

I'm glad he asked, because I was too stunned and grateful to do so myself.

Jonah looked at him blankly, so Heath went on to explain, 'Public Displays of Affection. How do you feel about Phoebe and me kissing etcetera in front of you?'

Jonah thought quietly for a few minutes. 'While it might be hard for me to witness at first, I think that more exposure I have to your own relationship with Phoebe, the more it will help me adjust to the reality of it. So please do not hesitate on my account.'

I was so thrilled by this resolution that I hugged and kissed them both.

'There is one last thing I would like to add,' Jonah said. 'Beyond our own close network of friends and family, I feel it would be most prudent to keep our *ménage à trois* secret. As far as anyone else is concerned, the two of you are the couple and you just happen to live with Heath's old man.'

'But I thought you were sick of hiding in the shadows?' I asked.

He gripped my thigh and grinned lasciviously. 'I felt that briefly, yes, but then I also enjoyed the thrill of sneaking around with you, Phoebe. I think it could help spice things up if we try it again.'

That cheeky smile did it for me every time. I

grabbed Jonah's hand and led him straight to the bedroom. 'Please excuse us, Heath.'

I faintly heard his reply, 'I don't mind one bit.'

Even though I was sure that Jonah closed the door behind us, halfway through our lovemaking I noticed that it was ajar. I just winked in the direction of the door before letting passion overwhelm me.

Chapter Thirty-Nine

Diary extract dated Wednesday 12th April 2006

'Do you know what today is, Phoebe?' he asked.

'Wednesday?' I suggested, teasingly.

'Well yes, but five years ago today was a Thursday, one that I will never forget.

Oh wow, he remembered!

'I have an anniversary gift for you, Phoebe.'

He produced a small gift box and handed it to me.

I t was Saturday night on April 8th in the year 2006. Life had been generally good to me in the intervening years. That's not to say that it was always easy. Living with two men, both my partners, posed some challenges from time-to-time, but we got through it overall.

Heath and I both completed our Bachelor Degrees with Honours and were due to graduate later that month. On this night, however, I was celebrating another great achievement: the publication of my first book, *From Prying Eyes*.

I was able to secure the Central Book Depository as my venue, with plenty of drinks and nibbles to keep the horde happy. When the time came for the formalities, Tom, my editor, called for everyone's attention. 'Good evening, all. I hope you have been enjoying yourselves so far. I would like to invite our newest author up front to say a few words. Phoebe Braddock, ladies and gentlemen.'

A round of applause followed as I took the spotlight, trembling slightly. 'Cheers, Tom. Hello everyone and thank you all for coming tonight. I would like to start with a few acknowledgements. Firstly, I want to thank my parents. Mum? Where are you?' I caught sight of my mum near the drinks table, along with her latest boyfriend, Trevor. I waved to her. 'My mother, Laura, ladies and gentlemen.'

This drew a cheer from the audience, and she blushed. I continued, 'I would not have gotten this far without her hard work and support. And my father, who many of you would know as adventure novelist, Tobias K. Braddock. Please step forward, Dad.' A much louder roar erupted from the crowd. 'I drew much of my inspiration and love of literature from this man, right from the beginning when he would attempt to read me the works of Tolkien—when I was just a toddler.' This evoked a few chuckles from people, Dad included.

I went on. 'Now there are two gentlemen here tonight who are very dear to me. Please join me up here, Heath and Jonah. I forbid these two men from opening their copies of the book until now. I would like to draw everyone's attention to the second page, which I will read to you all.'

They both stood beside me and opened their books. I opened my copy and read, 'I dedicate this novel to Heath and Jonah, who both taught me that love knows no boundaries.' The assembly cheered wildly, and Heath leaned in to kiss me. I also noticed Jonah tear up a little.

'Now for a few words on the book itself, if I may. I'm not going to lie to you all just to get more book sales. This will be a difficult read for some many people, I am sure. You may find it uncomfortable and confronting at times and I am sure it will challenge a lot of readers' values. But it is my hope that some people will come to understand and possibly even accept my message, because that would mean I have done just a little to help shift ideology in a less conservative direction.'

I then proceeded to read a short passage from the book.

After the launch, Jonah and Heath, both took me out for a private celebration at our favourite late-night dessert and cocktail bar. Somehow, I'd developed more of a sweet tooth in those few years since High School.

'You did very well up there, Phoebe. Both as your partner and former English teacher, I am incredibly proud of you,' Jonah smiled.

'I'm very proud of you too, babe,' Heath added.

I beamed. 'Thanks guys.'

Our cocktails arrived then, so Heath called for a toast. 'I think we ought to raise our glasses to Phoebe's book. May it fly off the shelves and have the readers begging for more.'

We clinked our glasses and cried, 'Cheers!'

Following the first round of drinks, Jonah bid us farewell. 'I am feeling quite tired now, Phoebe, so I am going to head home; but I want you to stay up and have more fun, okay?'

I was a little disappointed that he was bailing so soon. 'Are you sure you don't want me to come home with you?' I asked.

'I am sure. I am also quite happy for you to retire in Heath's bed for all of tonight.'

Now I was getting worried. *Had I upset him?* 'But why? Is something wrong?'

'Nothing is wrong, Phoebe. Please trust me on that. I just want to go to bed now.' He kissed me on the forehead, then briefly whispered something in Heath's ear before departing.

I turned to Heath and demanded, 'Okay, what the

hell's going on?'

Heath smiled and even blushed a little. 'Well there is something I wanted to talk to you about. Dad thought it best that I discuss this with you on my own.'

I waited with bated breath for him to continue.

'It hasn't escaped my notice, or Dad's, that you seem to have settled down a bit this last year. You haven't slept with anyone else outside of our home for what—ten months?'

I thought about it and agreed. 'I guess you're right. I just haven't felt the need to.'

He grinned widely. 'Have you noticed that you're not the only one who hasn't stepped outside in as many months?'

'Oh Wow! Now I think back… you haven't either.'

He reached for something in his jacket pocket, then spoke with a degree of anxiety in his voice. 'Which is why I feel that we might be ready… for the next step…'

Suddenly his was down on one knee.

Oh my God, was this really happening?

He opened a small Tiffany box to reveal an exquisite diamond ring. There were a few people at the neighbouring tables and all of them had turned to watch this spectacle. 'Before I ask the question, I want you to know that we have Dad's blessing and that your decision won't affect our *home arrangements*. So now, I am dying to know if you will marry me, Phoebe?'

I gaped, unable to find words. Marriage had never occurred to me before this point because I had always thought of it being more for conformists and religious types.

Heath was starting to look worried with how long I was taking to reply. So, I decided right then and there that I would define a new form of matrimony. 'Yes, I will marry you Heath!' I cried.

We embraced, then kissed passionately, only vaguely aware of the cheer from the crowd around us.

ॐ

The next day I drove straight over to see Denise. She had married Curtis during my second year of university, choosing me as her Maid of Honour. I found this little awkward and not just because of my previous views on marriage. Nick was the Best Man, and this was the first I had seen or heard of him since he'd left. I pushed on through because my support meant a lot to Denise, but Nick was not very friendly to me at any stage. After that day, he returned to Sydney without a word.

When Denise opened the door, I simply thrust my left hand out for her to see. She grabbed it, inspected the ring closely, then we both squealed like our old schoolgirl selves. 'It looks like one of those interlocking rings,' she observed.

'Yes, I guess he is saving the other half as the wedding band,' I said.

'Okay, but who proposed?' Denise was quite familiar with my domestic situation.

'Heath, of course. Jonah's still happy to *lurk in the shadows.*'

She brow furrowed. 'But what does this mean for you and Jonah?'

'Nothing much will change there. The main difference will be that Heath and I are committing to fooling around less.'

'Wow, you guys are like... so postmodern!'

I couldn't help but laugh.

Wednesday rolled around and Jonah greeted me enthusiastically after arriving home from work. He was still a High School teacher, although he stuck to boys' schools, mostly due to the flack he'd copped when he applied to return to St. Teresa's. I had been working on my latest book since eight in the morning and was quite ready to call it a day.

We sat down to a cup of tea, then Jonah asked, 'Did you get a message from Heath?'

I had been so caught up in my writing that day that I didn't even notice my phone. 'I don't know, I'll check now.'

Sure enough, there was a text from him: HI PHOEBE. I'M WORKING L8 2NIGHT, SOZ. ENJOY DINNER WITH DAD. ;-) XXX.

Heath had been fortunate to pick up a job with a

local television network, but it was proving to be very demanding at times.

'He sent me a similar message. I guess that means we have the place to ourselves tonight.' Jonah cooked an old favourite of ours that night, *filet de Poisson with gribiche salad*. I tried to help him in the kitchen, but he refused my attempts. 'I want you to sit and relax. Let me treat you tonight.'

I wondered what this was all in aid of.

After dinner, Jonah poured us some wine and we sat together on the couch. This was when he reminded me that it was essentially our five-year anniversary. He handed me the small gift box and I looked at him suspiciously. When I opened the box, I gasped.

Jonah explained, 'The ring that Heath proposed to you with was a sign of his commitment and promise to marry you. This is the other half of that ring, traditionally meant as the nuptial band, but there is nothing traditional about our situation. I feel that this ring symbolises the two of us and our continued commitment to each other. If you wear it alongside your engagement ring it will also signify the way our relationships are intertwined.'

He put it so eloquently. With tears in my eyes, I placed the ring next to its partner. 'Thank you.' Unable to express the full extent of my gratitude with words, I let my body do the talking.

Epilogue

Diary extract dated Thursday 26th May 2011

I sat there staring at the two lines on the test stick in momentary disbelief. I know that I haven't always been the best at taking my pill on time, but I'm still not prepared for this. We weren't planning for it; in fact, we haven't even talked about it.

Another five years on and I am now the happy wife of Mr. Heath Collins with Jonah my paramour. It took some time for Mum to come around to the idea of my polyandrous arrangement, but she eventually accepted it.

The day before I married Heath, we received a card in the mail from Sandra wishing the three of us well and apologising for her past behaviour. She said that it would have been nice to attend the wedding, but she understood why she was not invited. Heath and I have since reconciled with her and spent a week visiting her in the U.S, although Jonah never could forgive her.

Unfortunately, married life had not proven to be so joyful for Denise. Curtis wanted children, but she didn't and eventually this conflict drove them to divorce. Denise has since moved on from her secretarial work to pursue a successful career in hotel management. We remain best friends to this day.

Curtis' own vocation as a lawyer took off once they split and he recently settled down again with a female business partner. I still haven't heard from Nick, but I have seen him on television occasionally since he made it big as an actor.

As for Vince, well I found his trial challenging, especially when I was called as a witness and cross-examined regarding those two incidents. Thankfully, it all paid off when he was sentenced to life in prison on ten counts of rape along with drug-trafficking and even two counts of manslaughter.

Now I find myself writing my memoir in the hope that my unborn child will grow up an accepting and liberal-minded individual. It is also my wish that when they read this book, they will understand why the true identity of their biological father remains a mystery to all of us; but more importantly, why it doesn't matter. Heath and Jonah will both love him or her equally as their own.

What's Next?

Thank you for reading *I Heart Mr. Collins*. I would be most grateful if you could show your support by leaving a rating or even a review.

Phoebe's story ends here, but her writing does not. Check out her first novel, *From Prying Eyes*.

From Prying Eyes
A Phoebe Braddock Romance

Is the true expression of love really a sin?

Haunted by visions of a mysterious stranger making love to her in the dark, Sophie is torn between affections for the guy she's had a crush on for years and strong yearnings for the man of her dreams. And she can't shake the feeling that there is something familiar about her fantasy lover.

Then one fateful night, her dreams come to life at the debutante ball where Sophie is swept off her feet for several blissful minutes. But when the masks come off, she is forced to accept the shocking truth: her enigmatic lover is no stranger.

Does she deny her deepest desires or pursue a forbidden passion?

Note: This "spiritual successor" is the first novel that Phoebe wrote, and it can be read as a stand-alone.

AVAILABLE SEPTEMBER 2020

Keep reading for a sample...

Chapter One

The sound of a storm rumbling in the distance only enhanced Sophie's excitement and anxiety as she waited in the dark for her lover. She lay on her bed, dressed in a black satin slip. *What else could he teach me this time?* A sudden clap of thunder and the room lit up, then the sound of rain bucketing down. She chanced a brief look at the clock: 2AM already. He was late. She worried the weather had kept him away. *Should I remove the blindfold and attempt sleep?* A moment later, she heard someone opening her balcony door, the chill air touching her hot skin. Her heart skipped a beat before attempting to pound its way out of her rib cage. The door lock clicked, and the heat of the room intensified within seconds. He was upon her in a flash. Her mysterious stranger was with her at last. Her restricted sight enhanced her other senses. She could hear his fast, heavy breathing. She smelt his sandalwood cologne, which attempted to mask a more familiar scent she still couldn't place. Sophie tasted his salty lips as they pressed against hers; felt the stubble on his cheeks scratch her skin. She welcomed the touch of his calloused fingers as they explored her body, starting from her face and gradually working their way down. As they reached their destination, her senses blurred, then...

She awoke with a start, dripping with sweat, heart beating. It was always the same whenever she dreamt of sex. She never climaxed. *Is this because I have never been touched down there?* She looked over to the spare mattress on the floor. *Where is Candice?* Then she noticed the cool breeze entering her room. The balcony door was slightly ajar. *Odd.* She never left it open except for a summer heatwave. But it was mid-autumn in Victoria, Australia.

Sliding out of bed, she stepped into her slippers and crossed the room to the balcony. When she put her hand to the cold steel frame of the glass door, she noticed faint voices travelling on the wind, coming from her brother's room. *Was that a girl with him?* She threw on her dressing gown and crept outside, quietly following the terracotta tiled path to Stefan's door. She shivered a little in the brisk air, with its strong fragrance of pine trees from their Mediterranean style garden.

When she reached his room, she peered through the gap in the thick Tuscan curtains. *What the feck?* He was lying naked on the bed with *her* straddling him. *How could* she *do this to me?*

She remembered what Candice said at Stefan's

last gig: 'You know your brother's actually pretty hot.'

Sophie shrugged it off at the time. *Surely, Candice wouldn't break the code. But did she know the code?* A pang of jealousy gnawed at her while she watched them together. Stefan, her twin brother, had always been her best friend. Sophie often feared another girl coming between them, but he'd never found a girlfriend during their high school years. Candice was about to take his virginity. The first ever girl Sophie became close friends with was betraying her.

She should have left her vantage point and returned to bed, but Sophie was strangely intrigued by what was unfolding. At this point, it was literally the condom. Candice applied the rubber barrier with a deftness suggesting years of experience. Sophie was surprised by the considerable size of Stefan's erection. She'd seen him nude a few times since puberty, but it never looked like that!

My God, what's wrong with me? Why can't I look away? Sophie silently chided herself.

Candice was riding him, her hips thrusting with a force at odds with her fragile frame. Stefan's large, olive hands gripped her backside. They looked dark against her soft, pale skin. Candice applied a lot of makeup to her face to achieve the gothic pallor she wanted, yet the rest of her skin tone bore a close resemblance without cosmetics. Sophie had always admired her beauty; clearly, she wasn't alone!

They moved in a rhythmic unison; their breathing audible through the closed door. Hormones surged through Sophie's body. Subconsciously, she moved her left-hand to the moist area between her legs, slipped it inside her pyjama pants and thrummed the delicate skin with her fingers. When she caught herself plunging a finger deeper, she quickly withdrew, feeling ashamed. Mamma had always insisted masturbation was dirty and sinful, despite whatever else she heard.

The scene before her was coming to an end by this point. Candice groaned as she arched her back. Stefan gasped before screwing up his face, then Candice collapsed on him. Sophie quickly gathered her wits and dashed back to her room. Panting, she collapsed on her bed. She contemplated the private performance she'd witnessed. *Why am I aroused? Do I desire Candice? Surely it isn't because of my brother?*

⁎⁎⁎

Sophie touched the delicate Venetian mask pendant on its gold chain briefly as she finished getting dressed the following morning. She remembered Carnevale five years ago when Stefan had gifted it to her. Am I losing my dear, sweet brother? Snapping herself out of her reverie, she put the necklace on. It was the only item of jewellery she wore, feeling more comfortable in jeans and t-shirts than anything feminine. She brushed her long, wavy, brown hair, and quickly spritzed herself with some white musk perfume. She was ready to face the day.

The inviting smell of freshly brewed espresso and toast greeted Sophie as she descended the stairs for breakfast, running her hands along the smooth, polished wood atop the wrought iron railing.

Her mamma, Francesca, looked up from her conversation with Candice, smiling warmly as she entered the casual dining area. 'Ciao Sofia.'

'Ciao Mamma.' Sophie moved in and kissed her on both cheeks, carefully balancing her steaming hot espresso in her right-hand. She took her seat at the table, then greeted Candice timidly with a forced smile, 'Um, morning Candice.'

Her friend replied with a nod and a mouth half full of food, 'Hey.'

Sophie applied some marmalade to her toast, then dug in, using her meal to avoid conversation.

Mamma suddenly looked at the clock and frowned. 'Where's Stefano? He's gonna be-a late.'

Sophie noticed Candice stifle a smile. Both her lips and Sophie's remained sealed.

They resumed eating in silence until Papà swept into the room in his designer suit, filling the air with his overpowering citrus cologne and the rustling sound of papers. Attempting to close his overfull briefcase, he looked up and asked, 'Sofia, are you and your friend ready?'

'Sì, Papà—but Stefano?'

He glowered. 'Will have to catch the tram or drive himself.' Succeeding with the zip at last, he summoned them, 'Come.'

As if on cue, Stefan's dishevelled form stumbled through the door. Neither his short, undercut pompadour hair, nor his extended goatee had been groomed. He grinned at Candice briefly.

'*Stefano*!' Mamma cried. 'Why you make everyone late?'

'Sorry Mamma. Late night… studying.' He followed up with a kiss on Mamma's cheek, followed by Sophie's. 'Ciao Sofia.'

Papà scowled at him. 'Well I'm not waiting. You,' he pointed the leather case at Stefan, 'can find your own way. I'm already gonna be late for an important meeting.'

He poured the last of the coffee into his travel mug, then strode toward the garage. Sophie and Candice barely had time to grab their uni bags as they rushed after him.

∞CR

Sophie's ears were still ringing from the Italian opera that had blasted through the speakers of Papà's Audi. She looked at Candice as they alighted the pavement. *Was that drive as painful for her as it was for me?* If so, Candice didn't show any obvious signs of displeasure.

Sophie shivered in the crisp air as they walked across

the university campus, less enamoured by the hodgepodge of old gothic buildings and modern styles of architecture than usual. She tried to break the silence, 'So…d'ya get the reading done?'

Candice replied drily, 'Of course…I banged your brother last night by the way. Just thought you should know.'

Trying to act surprised, Sophie spun around to confront her friend, '*You did what*?'

Candice maintained her nonchalant composure. 'You heard me. I assume ya know what "banged" means?' She continued moving, urging Sophie forward again.

'Yes, but…' Sophie blinked in amazement.

The conversation was cut short once they reached the lecture hall. The drive from the Pacini family home in Toorak to the University of Melbourne during peak hour generally took between twenty to forty minutes. That morning the M1 was more congested than normal, making them late for Chemistry. After sneaking into the back row of the large, dimly lit auditorium, Sophie slumped into a chair and looked aghast at Candice. *How can she be so cool about this?* But Candice was too absorbed in their young Malaysian professor's talk on thermodynamics to notice.

৪০৫৪

Dominic pranced across the North Lawn to meet the

girls. He was in good spirits that day, likely due to the break in season. Cool weather meant clothing that had the dual effect of comfort and style. Embracing Sophie first, he exclaimed, 'Ciao bella!' Then they exchanged the customary kiss on the cheek. Turning to Candice he added, 'Hi Candice.' He didn't mind this strange goth who was following his bestie around, but it was hard to become close to someone as cold as the grave she'd apparently crawled out of.

Sophie commented, 'Hi Dom. Your accent's getting better. Those Italian classes are paying off.'

It was true that he had improved with the language since it became a university elective. During his high school years, most of his Italian vocab came from the bits he picked up around the Pacini household. He feigned insult in his reply: 'Thanks, Soph. I'll take that as a compliment.'

She pouted. 'I'm sorry, I didn't mean to imply…'

He cut her off. 'Nah, it's all good, really.' Pointing toward Union House, he continued, 'Shall we grab a bite? I'm famished.'

They made their way to a café for lunch. As they walked, he noticed Sophie glancing awkwardly at Candice a few times. *Have they been fighting?* They were lining up to order by this point and the delicious smell of pastries was making his stomach groan. Dominic, needing a distraction from hunger and unable to resist a good drama, inquired, 'Is something up with you two?'

It was Sophie who responded, 'Candice... took Stefan's V-card last night.'

Dominic couldn't believe his ears. 'Oh my God, Candice! You didn't, did you?'

Candice stared at him blankly. 'Yeh, but what's wrong with that?'

He was astounded as he cried, '*You broke the friendship code*!' Several startled students turned to look at him.

Candice asked, 'What's the "Friendship Code"?' She sounded so indifferent.

He sighed and rolled his eyes at her. 'Only like the most important unwritten rules of friendship *evah*.'

It was their turn to order. He promptly chose a goulash pie, fries, and a coffee. Once they were seated, he returned his attention to Candice. 'The "Friendship Code" says that we should never date or make moves on our friends' partners, ex-partners, or current crushes. It also says that we should ask permission before making moves on a friend's sibling.'

Candice gave him an incredulous eye. 'Sounds ridiculous to me. I can understand current partners or crushes, but the rest? Especially if you don't care about your exes anymore.'

A young man with blond, spiky hair and huge blue eyes delivered their food. He smiled at Dominic, which had him blushing slightly. They all dug in, giving them a moment of relative silence to think, amidst the din of the busy dining space.

Sophie sighed. 'I'm sorry Candice, but the thought of you with Stefan is weird.'

Dominic nodded with a mouth full of hot, juicy chunks of steak. After swallowing, he voiced his opinion. 'I agree. It's just too strange to talk about or even contemplate.'

Candice casually sipped her coffee then replied, 'Well don't think about it then. It's not like I was planning on telling you any details.'

Sick and angry with Candice, he didn't hide his disapproval when he asked, 'Does that mean you're just gonna go ahead and date Stefan anyway, despite Sophie's feelings?'

She answered in an amused tone, 'I never said anything about dating him. We had sex once. I can't promise it won't happen again, but I'm not interested in a committed relationship with him, or anyone else.'

Sophie seemed relieved then. 'I guess I can deal with that.'

Dominic wasn't pacified so easily; Candice's behaviour was outrageous in his opinion, but Stefan was Sophie's brother, not his. If Sophie was content, there was little more he could do. His lunch hour was coming to an end anyway. He stood up to give his farewell hug to Sophie. 'See you at Ballroom tonight, Soph?'

'Yes, of course. There's no way Mamma would let me miss it with my debut approaching.'

'Awesome. See you there. I've gotta get to my CAD class now.' He stormed off towards the computer suite without so much as a 'See Ya' to Candice.

೫೦೧

'Ciao Derrick.' Sophie hoped her greeting didn't sound too enthusiastic. This was her favourite Friday class because of him, and she was relieved to be free of Candice. She sat down in the noisy lecture hall, pulling her *Biology of Cells and Organisms* notebook and pen from her bag.

'Ciao Sofia.' He smiled with a slight curl to his full lips and sparkle in his brown, deep-set eyes, sending flutters through Sophie's nervous system.

Is he flirting with me, or am I getting my hopes up again? They had been mates for as long as she could remember. But this tall, muscular hunk of a Venetian with his black, choppy hair and swooped fringe was among the elites at school and she'd only ever been an oddball. It was nice having him as a friend, but that was as far as it ever went.

She attempted her own coy smile. Suddenly overcome by the warmth in the room, she commented, 'Wow. I think they've overdone the heating in here.'

Derrick eyed her with fascination. 'Yeh, I guess

they have.'

She stood up to remove a layer, sending her notebook flying into Derrick's lap and her pen to the floor. 'Shit! Sorry Derrick.' She quickly removed her grey knit jumper, then sat down.

Derrick was looking down at the open book in his lap with a grin. Sophie inspected the source of his amusement, then flushed. Her notes displayed a large diagram of the female reproductive system.

He looked back up into Sophie's eyes and his grin widened. 'Would you like to retrieve that, or should I *handle* it for you?'

This had to be flirting! Sophie decided to play along and smiled intently. 'Would you like to *handle* it for me?'

Derrick tittered. 'Certainly. But don't forget the pen. Should I grab *that* for you too?' He glanced down at the floor space by his foot.

The lecturer started talking at that moment and the chatter of the room hushed. Sophie leaned her head against Derrick's arm as she bent down for her pen, the tangy scent of his cologne invading her senses. She lingered a little, brushing her arm against the thick denim of his jeans as her fingers gripped their hard, plastic prize. He did not recoil at her touch. *This is a promising sign!*

With pen in hand, she gestured for her notebook. Derrick's index finger glided along the page, until it reached the section of the image marked 'Introitus,' then left it there a moment. He looked back into Sophie's eyes with a fierce intensity that made her own introitus quiver. *Is he testing me?* She refused to look away or betray her embarrassment. They remained locked in this holding pattern for a few minutes, then he ceded and returned the notebook.

Sophie tried to concentrate on the speaker up front, but his words washed over her. She was thinking about her neighbour and chanced the occasional look. It appeared that most glances went unnoticed, but he caught her once, halfway through the lecture. She hastily turned her gaze back to the front. When she looked back, his eyes were still fixed on her. He leered slightly before casually returning his attention to the lesson.

Sophie couldn't believe Derrick's conduct. *What had changed after all these years?* Her heart was pounding. *Should I try anything further?* She leaned in toward him slightly. He must have sensed her motive because he moved his arm across the back of her chair. *Oh my God! This is really happening!* She let her head rest against him. They remained in this sweet near-embrace for the remainder of the class.

When it was over, Derrick retrieved his arm and packed his bag. Sophie watched him hopefully.

Once finished, he spoke briefly, 'See ya in the prac on Monday.' He then stood up and left.

What the…? Was Derrick just teasing me? She packed her own belongings, then glumly made her way home.

Also By L. Starla

The Phoebe Braddock Books
(Taboo romance)

I Heart Mr. Collins
From Prying Eyes
Crystal's Crucible
Undeniably Wrong

Winter's Magic Series
(Urban fantasy / paranormal romance)

Winter's Maiden 1
Winter's Maiden 2
Winter's Thrall
Winter's Mother 1
Winter's Mother 2
Winter's Bride (TBA)
Winter's Crone 1 (TBA)
Winter's Crone 2 (TBA)

About the Author

Laelia Starla is an Australian author who was often found raiding her mother's shelves for any form of fiction she could get her hands on. Her first love was the horror genre, but she owes her passionate affair with the romance novel to her high-school English teacher, who got her hooked on the classics. Given her earlier reading, urban fantasy and paranormal romance seemed like a natural progression. Along with erotic romance, these have become her favourite genres to write.

Laelia also loves spending her spare time playing tabletop and video games, paper crafting, singing, dancing, and watching anime.

Access Exclusive Content

Join my newsletter to access free stuff like short stories, deleted scenes, fan art, and invitations to future launch events.

Newsletter: www.starlaarts.com>freebies

Follow me Online:
Website & Blog: www.starlaarts.com
Goodreads: 19660804.L_Starla
BookBub: www.bookbub.com/profile/l-starla
Amazon Author Profile: author/l.starla
Instagram: lstarlaauthor
Facebook: StarlaArts